Demon Thief

BOOK TWO
THE DEMONATA

DARREN SHAN

Demon Thief

HarperCollins *Children's Books*

Run with demons and find the thief on the web at
www.darrenshan.com

First published in hardback in Great Britain by HarperCollins *Children's Books* 2005
First published in paperback in Great Britain by HarperCollins *Children's Books* 2006
HarperCollins *Children's Books* is a division of HarperCollins *Publishers* Ltd
77-85 Fulham Palace Road, Hammersmith, London, W6 8JB

www.harpercollinschildrensbooks.co.uk

1

ISBN-13: 978 0 00 719323 3
ISBN-10: 0 00 719323 8

Printed and bound in England by
Clays Ltd, St Ives plc

INTO THE LIGHT

→People think I'm crazy because I see lights. I've seen them all my life. Strange, multicoloured patches of light swirling through the air. The patches are different sizes, some as small as a coin, others as big as a cereal box. All sorts of shapes — octagons, triangles, decagons. Some have thirty or forty sides. I don't know the name for a forty-sided shape. *Quadradecagon?*

No circles. All of the patches have at least two straight edges. There are a few with curves or semi-circular bulges, but not many.

Every colour imaginable. Some shine brightly, others glow dully. Occasionally a few of the lights pulse, but normally they just hang there, glowing.

When I was younger I didn't know the lights were strange. I thought everybody saw them. I described them to Mum and Dad, but they thought I was playing a game, seeking attention. It was only when I started school and spoke about the lights in class that it became an issue. My teacher, Miss Tyacke, saw that I wasn't making up stories, that I really believed in the lights.

Miss Tyacke called Mum in. Suggested they took me to somebody better qualified to understand what the lights signified. But Mum's never had much time for psychiatrists. She thinks the brain can take care of itself. She asked me to stop mentioning the lights at school, but otherwise she wasn't concerned.

So I stopped talking about the lights, but the damage had already been done. Word spread among the children — Kernel Fleck is *weird*. He's not like us. Stay away from him.

I never made many friends after that.

→My name's Cornelius, but I couldn't say that when I was younger. The closest I could get was Kernel. Mum and Dad thought that was cute and started using it instead of my real name. It stuck and now that's what everybody calls me.

I think some parents shouldn't be allowed to name their kids. There should be a committee to forbid names which will cause problems later. I mean, even without the lights, what chance did I have of fitting in with any normal crowd with a name like Kernel – *or* Cornelius – Fleck!

We live in a city. Mum's a university lecturer. Dad's an artist who also does some freelance teaching. (He actually spends more time teaching than drawing, but whenever anyone asks, he says he's an artist.) We live on the third floor of an old warehouse which has been converted into apartments. Huge rooms with very high ceilings. I sometimes feel like a Munchkin, or Jack in the giant's castle.

Dad's very good with his hands. He makes brilliant model aeroplanes and hangs them from the wooden beams of my bedroom ceiling. When they start to clutter the place up, or if we just get the urge one lazy Sunday afternoon, the pair of us make bombs out of apples, conkers – whatever we can find that's hard and round – and launch them at the planes. We fire away until we run out of ammo or all the planes are destroyed. Then Dad sets to work on new models and we do it all over again. At the moment the ceiling's about a third full.

I like it here. Our apartment is great; we're close to lots of shops, a cool adventure playground, museums, cinemas galore. School's OK too. I don't make friends, but I like my teachers and the building — we have a first-rate lab, a projection room, a massive library. And I never get beaten up — I roar automatically when I'm fighting, which isn't good news for bullies who don't want to attract attention!

But I'm not enjoying life. I'm lonely. I've always been a loner, but it didn't bother me when I was younger. I liked being by myself. I read lots of books and comics, watched dozens of TV shows, invented imaginary friends to play with. I was happy.

That changed recently. I don't know why, but I don't like being alone now. I feel sad when I see groups of friends having a good time. I want to be one of them. I want friends who'll tell me jokes and laugh at mine, who I can discuss television shows and music with, who'll pick me to be on their team. I try getting to know people, but the harder I try, the more they avoid me. I sometimes hover at the edge of a group, ignored, and pretend I'm part of it. But if I speak, it backfires. They glare at me suspiciously, move away or tell me to get lost. "Go watch some lights, freak!"

The loneliness got really bad this last month. Nothing interests me any more. The hours drag, especially at home or when I have free time at school. I can't distract myself. My mind wanders. I keep thinking about friends and how I don't have any, that I'm alone and might always be. I've talked with Mum and Dad about it, but it's hard to make them understand how miserable I am. They say things will change when I'm older, but I don't believe them. I'll still be weird, whatever age I am. Why should people like me more then than now?

I try so hard to fit in. I watch the popular shows and listen to the bands I hear others raving about. I read all the hot comics and books. Wear trendy clothes when I'm not at school. Swear and use all the cool catchphrases.

It doesn't matter. Nothing works. Nobody likes me. I'm wasting my time. This past week, I've got to thinking that I'm wasting my entire life. I've had dark, horrible thoughts, where I can only see one way out, one way of stopping the pain and loneliness. I know it's wrong to think that way – life can never be *that* bad – but it's hard not to. I cry when I'm alone — once or twice I've even cried in class. I'm eating too much food, putting on weight. I've stopped washing and my skin's got greasy. I don't care. I want to look like the freak I feel I am.

→Late at night. In bed. I'm playing with the patches of light, trying not to think about the loneliness. I've always been able to play with the lights. I remember being three or four years old, the lights all around me, reaching out and moving them, trying to fit them together like jigsaw pieces. Normally, the lights remain at a distance of several feet, but I can call them closer when I want to play with them.

The patches aren't solid. They're like floating scraps of plastic. If I look at a patch from the side, it's almost invisible. I can put my fingers through them, like ordinary pools of light. But, despite that, when I want to move a patch, I can. If I focus on a light, it glides towards me, stopping when I tell it. Reaching out, I push at one of the edges with my fingers. I don't actually touch it, but as my fingers get closer, the light moves in whatever direction I'm pushing. When I stop, the light stops.

I figured out very early on that I could put patches together to make patterns. I've been doing it ever since, at night, or during lunch at school when I have nobody to play with. Lately, I've been playing with them more than ever. Sometimes, the lights are the only way I have to escape the miserable loneliness.

I like making weird shapes, like Picasso paintings. I saw a programme on him at school a couple of years ago and felt an immediate connection. I think Picasso saw lights too, only he didn't tell anyone. People wouldn't have thought he was a great artist if he said he saw lights — they'd have said he was a nutcase, like me.

The shapes I make are nowhere near as fabulous as Pablo Picasso's paintings. I'm no artist. I just try to create interesting designs. They're rough, but I like them. They never last. The shapes hold for as long as I'm studying them, but once I lose interest, or fall asleep, they come undone and the pieces drift apart, returning to their original positions in the air around me.

The one I'm making tonight is particularly jumbled. I'm finding it hard to concentrate. Joining the pieces randomly, with no real purpose. It's a mess. I can't stop thinking about not having any friends. Feeling wretched. Wishing I had at least one true friend, someone who'd care about me and play with me, so I wasn't completely alone.

As I'm thinking about that, a few of the patches pulse. No big deal. Lights have pulsed before. Usually, I ignore them. But tonight, sad and desperate to divert my train of thought, I summon a couple, study them with a frown, then put them together and call for the rest of the flashing patches. As I add those pieces to the first two, more lights pulse, some slowly, some quickly.

I sit up, working with more speed. This new flashing shape is curious. I've never put pulsing patches together before. As I add to the cluster, more lights pulse. I quickly slot them into place, working as if on autopilot. I have no control over myself. I keep watching for a pattern to emerge, but there isn't one. Just a mass of different pulsing colours. Still, it's worked its magic. I'm focused on the cluster of lights now, dark thoughts and fears temporarily forgotten.

The lights build and build. This is a massive structure, much larger than any I've previously created. I'm sweating and my arms are aching. I want to stop and rest, but I can't. I'm obsessed with the pulsing lights. This must be what addiction is like.

Then, without warning, the patches that I've stuck together stop pulsing and all glow a light blue colour. I fall back, gasping, as if I'd got an electric shock. I've never seen this happen. It scares me. A huge blue, jagged patch of light at the foot of my bed. It's like a window. Large enough for a person to fit through.

My first thought is to flee, call for Mum and Dad, get out as quick as I can. But part of me holds firm. An inner voice whispers in my ear, telling me to stay. *This is your window to a life of wonders*, it says. *But be careful*, it adds, as I move closer to the light. *Windows open both ways.*

As it says that, a shape presses through, out of the panel of light. A face. I'm too horrified to scream. It's a monster from my very worst nightmare. Pale red skin. A pair of dark red eyes. No nose. A small mouth. Sharp, grey teeth. As it leans further forward into my bedroom, I see more of it and the horror intensifies. It doesn't have a heart! There's a hole in the left side of its chest, but where the heart should be are dozens of tiny, hissing snakes.

The monster frowns and stretches a hand towards me. I can see more than two arms — at least four or five. I want to pull away. Dive beneath my bed. Scream for help. But the voice that spoke to me a few seconds ago won't let me. It whispers quickly, words I can't follow. And I find myself standing firm, taking a step towards the panel of light and its emerging monster. I raise my right hand and watch the fingers curl into a fist. I can feel a strange tingling sensation, like pins and needles.

The monster stops. Its eyes narrow. It looks round my bedroom uncertainly. Then slowly, smoothly, it withdraws, pulling back into the panel of light, vanishing gradually until only its red eyes remain, staring out at me from within the surrounding blueness, twin circles of an unspoken evil. Then they're gone too and I'm alone again, just me and the light.

I should be wailing for help, running for my life, cowering on the floor. But instead my fingers relax and my fist unclenches. I'm facing the panel of blue light, staring at it like a zombie transfixed by a fresh human brain, distantly processing information. Normally, the patches of light are transparent, but I can't see through this one. If I look round it, there's my bedroom wall, a chest of drawers, toys and socks scattered across the floor. But when I look directly at the light, all I see is blue.

The voice says something crazy to me. I know it's madness as soon as it speaks. I want to argue, roar at it, tell it to get stuffed. But, as scared and confused as I am, I can't disobey. I find my legs tensing. I know, with sick certainty, what's going to happen next. I open my mouth to scream, to try and stop it, but before I can, a force makes me step forward — after the monster, into the light.

FUGITIVES

→Next thing I know, I'm on the floor of my bedroom, my baby brother Art cradled to my chest. Mum and Dad are shouting at me, crying, poking and clutching me. Dad gently takes Art from my arms. Mum crouches beside me and hugs me hard, weeping over my bald skull. She's moaning, calling my name over and over, asking where I've been, what happened, if I'm all right. Dad's staring at me like I've got two heads, only looking away to check on Art, his expression one of total bewilderment.

There's no panel of blue light. No monster. And no memory of what happened when I stepped through after the snake-hearted creature.

→I learn that I've been missing for several days. Mum and Dad thought I'd been kidnapped, or wandered out and got lost. The police have been searching for me. They put my photo in newspapers and questioned all the people who knew me. Mum and Dad were frantic. Mum keeps weeping, saying she thought I was dead, that she'd lost another of her babies. I don't like the way she refers to me as a baby, but this isn't the time to correct her!

I can't remember what happened. Up to the moment I took that step forward into the blue light — total recall. After that — nothing.

Mum and Dad don't believe me. They think I'm lying or in shock. They ply me with hot chocolate in our kitchen and quiz me ruthlessly, sometimes gently, sometimes harshly, neither of them in complete control of themselves. They pass Art back and forth, asking me questions about how he ended up with me. I guess he must have gone missing too, after I did.

"Can I hold Art?" I ask, during a brief lull in the questioning.

Mum passes him to me, watching us suspiciously, perhaps afraid we'll go missing again. I had a younger sister once — Annabella. She died when she was a baby. I can't remember much about her — I was only four. But I'll never forget Mum and Dad's tears, the misery, the loss I sensed in the air around me. I wasn't much more than a baby myself, but I knew something terrible had happened, and I could see how upset Mum and Dad were. I guess they never really got over that. It's only natural that they're more upset and worried now than most parents would be.

I bounce Art up and down on my knee, cooing to him, telling him everything's OK. "You're my little brother. I'll look after you. It's fine." He doesn't take much notice. He looks more sleepy than afraid. Too young to catch the bad vibes.

Mum and Dad stare at each other wordlessly then leave us alone for a while, going out into the corridor to discuss the situation. They don't shut the door behind them, and call out to me whenever I stop talking to Art, making sure we're still here.

→They let me go to bed at one in the morning. Their faces are strained and red. Mum tucks me in and lets Art sleep beside me. She rubs his face tenderly as she pulls the blanket up around him. Starts to cry again. Dad tugs her away, kisses me, then takes Mum back to their bedroom, leaving me and Art to sleep.

→I wake in the middle of the night. Mum and Dad are arguing. I don't know what about. Mum's saying, "Let's give it a few days. Watch. Wait. If nobody says anything, or looks for him…"

Dad shouts, "You're crazy! We can't! It's wrong! What if the police…?"

I drift back to sleep.

→Morning. More questions. Mum sits Art on her lap and feeds him, smiling and laughing wildly every time he gurgles at her. It's a good job I'm not jealous of my little brother as she hardly notices I'm here.

Dad's upset. He keeps glaring at Mum and Art. Throws more questions at me. Tries to help me unlock my memories. Asks me to take him through the night I vanished, step by step. I tell him I was in my bedroom, I was playing and that's all I remember. I don't mention the lights or the monster. The inner voice that spoke to me that night tells me not to. Says I'd only get into more trouble if I told the truth.

"Did you go to bed?" Dad asks.

"No."

"Did someone come into the room?"

"No."

"Was there somebody at the window?"

A pause while I think back. "No."

"What about… Art? Can you remember where… how you got him?"

"No."

He curses and tugs at his hair with both hands. Looks at Mum and Art again. Mum stares back at him sternly, holding Art against her like a shield. I don't know what her look means, but I'm glad she's not looking at me that way — her eyes are scary!

→Dad phones the police and they come round. He sits with me while they ask lots of questions. Mum stays in their bedroom with Art. Dad said there was no need to talk about Art with the police. It would only complicate things. Since

Art's too young to tell them anything, they want to focus on what happened to me.

I tell the police the same things I told Mum and Dad. The police are nice. They talk softly, make jokes, tell me stories about other kids who were lost or kidnapped. They want to know if I remember anything, even the smallest detail, but my mind is a complete blank. I keep apologising for not being able to tell them anything more, but they don't lose patience. They're much calmer than Mum and Dad.

→I don't go back to school. Mum and Dad keep me in. Won't even let me go out to the park. Things feel strange and awkward. It's like when Annabella died. Lots of crying, sorrow and uncertainty. But it's different. There's fear too. Mum's especially edgy. Hardly lets go of Art. Snaps at Dad a lot of the time. I often find her shaking and crying when she doesn't think I'll notice.

→Days pass. The police come back, but they're not too worried. The most important thing is that I'm safe and back home. They recommend a good psychiatrist to Dad, and suggest he takes me to see her, to try and figure out what happened to me. Dad says he will, but I remember what Mum was like when Miss Tyacke suggested a psychiatrist all those years ago. I'm sure I won't be going for counselling.

→That night they have a huge row. Mum's screaming and cursing. I'm in my room with Art. They think we can't hear them, but we can. I'm scared. I even cry a bit, holding Art tightly, not sure why they're behaving this way. Art's not bothered. He gurgles happily in my arms and tries biting a hole through the new bib that Dad bought yesterday.

Mum yells, "We've been given a second chance! I don't care how it happened or who gets hurt! I'm not going to suffer the loss of a child again!"

I can't hear Dad's reply, but it seems to do the trick. Mum doesn't shout after that, though I hear her crying later. I hear Dad crying too.

→The next morning, Dad calls me into his study. He has Art on one knee, a picture of Annabella on the other. He's looking from Art to the picture and back again, chewing his lower lip. He looks up when I enter and smiles — a thin, shaky smile. Tells me we're leaving. Immediately, this very night.

"We're going on holiday?" I ask, excited.

"No. We're moving house." Art tugs at Dad's left ear. Dad ducks his head and chuckles at Art. "Your Mum doesn't like it here any more," Dad says quietly, not looking at me directly. "Annabella died here. You went missing. Art… well, she doesn't want anything else to happen. To Art or to you. She wants to go somewhere safer. To be honest, I do too. I'm sick of city life."

"But what about school?" It's the first question to pop into my head.

"The hell with it," Dad laughs. "You don't like it that much, do you?"

"Well… no… but it's my school."

"We'll find you another." He fixes Art in his left arm, then extends his right and pulls me in close. "I know you haven't been happy here. Mum and I have been thinking about it. We're going to move to a place we know, a village called Paskinston. The children will be very different there. Nicer than city kids. We think you'll be happier, maybe make some friends. And you'll be safe. We all will. How does that sound?"

"Good. I guess. But…" I shrug.

"It's for the best, Kernel," Dad says and hugs me tight. Art laughs and hugs me too, and that's when I feel sure that Dad's right. Everything's going to be better now.

→My last glimpse of the city is when I get into our car late that night. I don't know why we don't wait until morning – Dad hates driving at night – but I haven't had time to ask. It's been a rush, packing bags, going through all of my toys, books, comics, clothes, records, choosing what to bring and what to leave behind. Dad says we'll get the rest of our belongings sent on later, but I don't want to leave anything precious behind, just in case. I bombed all of the planes in my bedroom at 9 o'clock. Mum and Dad helped me. We destroyed them completely. It was cool! Even Mum enjoyed it.

As we're getting into the car, Dad asks if I want to play a game with Art, to keep him quiet. I say sure. So he makes me sit on the floor behind Mum's seat, with Art between my legs, and he drapes a blanket over us. "Pretend Art and you are fugitives. You're a pair of vicious, wanted criminals and we're sneaking you out of the city. There are roadblocks, so you have to hide and be quiet. If you're found, you'll be sent to prison."

"Children don't get sent to prison!" I snort.

"They do in this game," Dad laughs.

I know it's just a way for Mum and Dad to keep Art — and me — quiet for some of the journey. But part of me thinks it's real. The fact that we're leaving so quickly, at night, in secrecy... I hold Art tight in my arms and whisper for him to be quiet, afraid we'll be caught by whoever's after us. I feel like crying, but that's because we're leaving home. I've never lived anywhere else. It's scary.

Mum checks that Art and I are OK before getting in the car. She lifts the blanket and peers in at us. We're parked close to a street light, so I can see her face pretty well. She looks worried — maybe she's sad to be leaving our old home, like me.

"Take care of your brother," she says softly, stroking Art's left cheek. He gazes at her quietly. "Protect him," Mum says, her voice cracking. Then she kisses my forehead, replaces the blanket and we set off, leaving behind everything I've ever known.

THE WITCH

→Paskinston's a sleepy place, with a couple of tiny shops, a crumbling old school, a stumpy, ugly, modern church, and not much else. It's in the middle of nowhere, miles away from any town or city. Power cuts are common. Television and radio reception is poor. Cars are mostly ancient wrecks. The sort of place where you expect to find loads of old people, but in fact most of the villagers are youngish parents and their children.

We've been here almost a year. It's not a bad place to live. Quiet and clean. Lots of open space around the village. No pollution or crime, and people are very relaxed and friendly. A few commute to cities or towns, but most work locally. Quite a few are craftspeople and artists. We don't get many tourists in Paskinston, but our artisans (as Dad calls them) supply a lot of tourist shops around the country. Musical instruments are the village's speciality, traditionally carved, lovingly created and packaged, then expensively priced!

Dad's got a job painting instruments. It doesn't pay very well, but you don't need much money in Paskinston. He's happier than he ever was in the city, finally able to call himself a real artist. Mum helps out kids with learning problems, and does some teaching in the school when one of the regular teachers is off sick. She's happy too, the happiest I've seen her since Annabella died.

Mum and Dad never talk about the time Art and I went missing. It's a forbidden subject. If I ever bring it up, they change the topic immediately. Once, when I pressed, Mum snapped at me, swore and told me never to mention it again.

And me? Well, I'm OK. Dad was right. The kids here *are* nicer than in the city. They chat to me at school, include me in their games, invite me to their houses to read and play, take me on day trips into the local countryside at weekends. Nobody bullies me, says nasty things to me or tries to make me feel like I'm a freak. (Of course, it helps that I don't mention the secret patches of light!)

But I still don't fit in. I feel out of place. It's hard to talk freely, to join in, to behave naturally. I always feel as though I'm acting. Most of the kids in Paskinston were born here or moved here when they were very young. This is the only world they know and they believe it's perfect.

I don't agree. While I'm certainly happier now than I was in the city, I miss the cinemas and museums. Except for not having any friends, I liked being part of a big city, where there was always something new to see or do. The village is nice, but it's a bit boring. And although the kids are nicer to me, I still haven't made any real friends.

But it's not that important because I'm not miserable any more. I'm not sure why, but I don't feel lonely these days. I'm happy just to be with Mum, Dad and Art. Especially Art. He might only be a baby, but I love dragging him around with me, explaining the world to him, telling him about books, television and life, trying to teach him to speak. He should have started by now, but so far not a word. Dad and Mum don't mind. They say Einstein was older than Art is before he spoke. But I don't think Art's an Einstein — he likes tugging ears, biting people and burping too much to be a genius!

Art's all I really need from the world right now. He keeps me company better than any friend ever could. As Dad once said when I was lonely and he was trying to cheer me up, "Who needs friends when you have family?"

→To get to school, I have to pass the witch's house.

The "witch" is Mrs Egin. There are thirty-seven families and six single people in Paskinston, and everyone's on friendly terms with everybody else. There's a real sense of community. They all take an interest in and see a lot of each other, chat among themselves when they meet in the street or at church, hold big parties every few months to which everyone comes.

Except Mrs Egin. She lives by herself in a dirty old house and almost never has anything to say to anybody. She comes out for a long walk every day and to draw water from the well. (There's running water in Paskinston, but Mrs Egin and a few others prefer to get theirs from an old well in the centre of the village.) But otherwise we rarely see her. She spends most of her time indoors, behind thick curtains, doing whatever it is that witches do.

I'm sure she's not really a witch, but all the kids call her the Pricklish Witch of Paskinston. Some of the adults do too!

There isn't a real school in Paskinston, just a converted stable which is being used as a school until the villagers manage to build a proper one. There are three teachers (two are volunteers), crappy old desks, wobbly chairs, a few tired blackboards, and nothing else except the ancient toilets out the back. A big change from my school in the city!

The school's down the street and round the corner to the left from where we live. To get there, I have to walk past Mrs Egin's house. I could go the opposite way and circle round the backs of the houses if I wanted. But Mrs Egin has never done anything bad to me. She hasn't even spoken to me in the year that I've lived here. She doesn't frighten me.

Today, I set off for school as normal. Classes start at 9:30 a.m. but I normally get there for 9 o'clock, to play some games with the other kids beforehand. Trying hard to fit in, to be like they are, to have them accept me. Not that I'm too bothered if they don't.

"Off to school?" Mum asks as I'm heading out.

"Yes."

"Want to take Art to the crèche?"

"Sure."

The makeshift crèche is in another converted stable, right next to the school. I often drop Art off.

Art's small and skinny. A large head though. Dad says that's a sign that he has lots of brains, but I think it's because he has a thick skull — all the better for headbutting!

I stop Art trying to bite the hands off a soldier doll and pick him up. He struggles, eager to finish off the soldier. "Stop," I grunt. Art calms down immediately. He always does what I tell him. He's more obedient for me than for Mum or Dad. Mum says that's a sign that he really loves me. It makes me proud when she says stuff like that, though I usually scowl — don't want her thinking I'm soft.

Art's pale, like Mum, with dirty dark hair that looks like it's never been washed. Mum always complains about Art's hair. She regularly threatens to shave him bald like me. (Not that *I* need to shave — I've been bald since birth.) She says every guy should be bald — it makes life much simpler for the women looking after them.

I throw Art up in the air and catch him. He laughs and gurgles for me to do it again. I compare my skin to his as I toss him up a second time. I'm much darker, a nice creamy brown, more Dad's colour than Mum's. We don't look like brothers. Mum says that's good — people won't confuse us when we're older.

I settle Art down and head for the door, carrying him under one arm like a skateboard. He swings his fists around, looking for something to hit. He almost never hits or bites me, but I'm the only one who's safe around him. He's given Mum a black eye a few times and bit one of Dad's fingernails off once. He'll be a real terror when he's a couple of years older.

We set off down the street. There's nobody else around. A quiet spring day. Birds are twittering in the trees. A cow moos in the distance. I feel warm and happy. Looking forward to summer. Dad said we might go to the beach for a week or two. We haven't been on a holiday since we left the city. I'm excited about it.

"You've never seen a beach, have you?" I say to Art. "It's great. More sand than you could imagine. Salt water, not like the ponds here. Seaweed. We can swim and make sandcastles. Eat ice cream and candyfloss. You'll love it. And if we can't go, well, we'll camp round here instead. Find a lake, maybe near a small town, with a cinema and amusement arcades and–"

"*Thief!*" someone screeches.

We've just passed the witch's house. I look back. The front door's open. Mrs Egin is standing on the doorstep. Her eyes are wild and she's trembling. Her hair's normally tied in a ponytail, but today it's hanging loose, strands blowing across her face in the light breeze.

"Who's the thief?" she mutters, staggering towards me.

"Mrs Egin? Are you all right? Do you want me to fetch help?" I set Art down to my left and step in front of him, shielding him with my legs, in case she falls on top of him.

Mrs Egin stops less than a foot away. She's mumbling to herself, strange words, no language that I know. Her lips are bleeding — she's bitten through them in several places. Her fingers are wriggling like ten angry snakes.

"Mrs Egin?" I say softly, heart racing.

"Such a beautiful baby," the witch says, eyes fixed on Art. He's staring up at her silently. Mrs Egin bends and reaches for Art, cooing, smiling crookedly.

"Leave him alone," I gasp, shuffling Art back with my left foot, standing firmly in front of him now, blocking her way.

"Not yours!" she snarls, glaring at me. I've never seen an adult look at me that way, with total hate. It scares me. I feel like I have to pee. Clench my legs together so I don't have an accident.

But, scared as I am, I don't move. I stand my ground. I have to protect Art.

"Are you ill, Mrs Egin?" I ask, my voice a lot calmer than I feel.

"Find him!" she shouts in reply. "Find the thief! Beautiful baby." She smiles at Art again, then mumbles to herself, like a minute ago, but gesturing at Art this time, as though she's casting a spell on him.

I look for help but we're all alone. I can't just stand here and let this go on. No telling what she'll do next. So, without taking my eyes off her, I stoop, grab Art and awkwardly hold him up behind my back. Art squeals happily — he thinks I'm giving him a piggyback ride.

"We have to go now," I say, edging away. Mrs Egin's still looking at the spot where Art was. I notice that lots of the patches of light around us are pulsing. They're closer than they normally are, as if hedging us in. But I can't worry about the lights. Not with Mrs Egin acting like a real, mad witch.

"Soon!" Mrs Egin barks and her eyes snap upwards. "All be happening soon. They thought I didn't have it in me. Said I was weak. But they were wrong. I have the power. I can serve." Her hands go still. Her eyes soften. "You will see me die," she says quietly.

Tears of confusion and fear come to my eyes. "Mrs Egin, I... I'll fetch help... I'll get someone who can—"

"Thief!" she yells, silencing me, wild and twisted again. Her hands come up and wave angrily at me. "Find the thief! Soon! You'll see. The mad old witch going up in a puff of smoke. Boom, Kernel Fleck. *Boom!*"

She laughs hysterically. When you hear a witch laugh in a movie, it's funny. But this isn't. The laughter hurts my ears, makes them ring from deep inside. I half expect them to start bleeding.

"I have to go now," I say quickly, turning away from her, sliding Art round so he's in front of me, all the time protecting him from her.

"Kernel," the witch says in a cold, commanding tone. Reluctantly, I stop and look back. "You won't tell anyone what you've seen today." It's not a question.

"Mrs Egin… you need help… I think…"

She spits on the ground by her right foot. "You're a fool. I'm not the one who needs help — *you* are. But never mind that. You won't tell anyone. Because if you do, I'll creep into your room late at night when you're asleep and slit your throat from your left ear to your right." She uses a trembling index finger to illustrate.

That's too much. I lose control and, to my shame, feel the front of my trousers go wet. Fortunately Mrs Egin doesn't see. She's already turned away. Walks back to her house. Pauses at the front door. Looks up. There's a six-sided patch of pink light pulsing rapidly just above her head. She reaches up and strokes it. The pulse rate slows, as if the light was afraid and she has calmed it down.

"Thought you were the only one who could see them," she says as I stare at her in shock. "But I can too. Now. For a while. Until they take me."

Then she goes inside and shuts the door.

For a long moment I stand, fighting back tears, ears still ringing, wanting to run away and never return. But I can't do that, and I can't turn up at school with wet, stained trousers. So I hurry home, clutching Art tight to my chest, steering as far wide of the witch's house as I can.

MARBLES

→I lie to Mum. Tell her Art peed on me. She's surprised — he's never been a wetter. She wants to change him. I tell her it's all right, I'll take care of it. I hurry to my bedroom and change my trousers. I'm almost out the door before I remember that Art should be changed too, so I quickly find clean clothes for him.

I consider telling Mum about Mrs Egin's behaviour. Recall her threat — "slit your throat from your left ear to your right." Don't say a word.

→The day passes uncomfortably. I can't forget what Mrs Egin said, her wicked expression, stroking the pulsing patch of light. "You will see me die."

I should tell someone. It doesn't matter that she threatened me. She won't be able to sneak into my room if I tell someone and they lock her up like the mad old witch she is.

But I wet my trousers. If I tell about the rest, I'll have to tell about that too. And I don't want people knowing. So I say nothing. I pretend it didn't happen, that it doesn't matter. And all day long I feel as if a thousand eels of terror are wriggling around inside me.

→Dad's talking with Mum about a craft fair when I come home. She's listening quietly, sitting by the piano. (It was in the house when we moved in — none of us can play.) She's frowning.

"This is one of the biggest fairs in the country," Dad says. "It's held every year, and a few of the Paskinston artists always go, representing the village. They sell a lot of work at it and rack up loads of orders. It's a real honour to be asked. It would be rude to refuse."

"But can't one of us go and one stay here?" Mum asks.

"Yes, but couples normally go together. It's not just about selling. There are hundreds of artists and interesting people there. It's a chance to meet, mingle, get to know other people. It'll be fun."

I hand Art to Mum and sit close to her, following the conversation. I learn a bit more about the fair, where it's held, who's going, how long they'll be gone for. Dad's proud to have been invited and keen to go, but Mum's worried about Art and me. She doesn't want to leave us alone. "Can't we take them along?" she asks.

"It's not the done thing," Dad says patiently. "Nobody else brings their kids."

Mum's frown deepens. We haven't been apart since we

left the city, not for a single night. But if they go to the fair, they'll be gone for at least a week.

"They won't be by themselves," Dad says. "We'll leave them with one of the neighbours."

"I know, but…"

"Kernel doesn't mind. Do you, Kernel?" He smiles broadly at me, expecting my support. If this was yesterday, I'd have given it instantly. But Mrs Egin's threat is fresh in my thoughts. I don't want to be left alone. So I just shrug in answer. "You OK, big guy?" Dad asks, surprised.

"Yeah."

"If you don't want us to go, just say. It's not *that* important."

"No. I mean, I don't mind. Not really. It's just…" I can't explain without telling them the truth. So again I shrug.

"What about Art?" Mum says, kissing his head, looking up at Dad.

"Art will be fine too," Dad says and he sounds a little impatient now.

"I'm not sure, Caspian."

"Melena…" Dad sighs. "Look, if it's going to be a big deal, we won't go. But this is our home now. We're safe here. I don't think we've anything to fear in this place. Do you?"

"No," Mum says quietly.

"So…?"

Mum pulls a face. "I just don't like being apart from my darling babies!" she exclaims. We all laugh at that, and everything's fine again. Mum bounces Art up and down on her knee. Dad smiles and hugs her. I feel happy and safe. I ask what's for dinner, and forget about the witch and all the bad thoughts of the day.

→The morning of their departure. Dad gets the car ready while Mum takes Art and me over to Sally's house. Sally is one of the villagers who lives alone. A bit older than Mum. Fat. A great singer. She has two children of her own, but they've grown up and left.

"We're going to have a great time," Sally says as we set our bags down in the room where Art and I are staying.

"I wish there was a phone, so we could call and check that everything is all right," Mum grumbles. There aren't many phones in the village and Sally doesn't own one.

"Relax!" Sally laughs. "These boys can get along fine without you for a few days. Can't you, Kernel?"

"Sure," I smile. Mum smiles back, but shakily.

Dad calls us and we head out. He's standing by the car. The back seat and boot are filled with musical instruments and paintings. Two other couples have already left in a caravan with the majority of the pieces which they hope to sell. Dad hugs Art, then me.

"Look after your brother," Mum says, kissing my cheek.

"Of course he will," Dad says. "Kernel's the best brother in the world. He'll take care of Art better than you or I could."

Dad gets in and starts the engine. Mum hugs us one last time, then sits in beside him. And they're off. Art, Sally and I wave after them. Mum rolls down her window, leans out and waves back, until they turn a corner. Although Sally's right beside us, I can't help but think as they roll out of sight — we're alone now. Just Art and me. In a remote village. With a witch.

→The day passes smoothly. School, playing with Art during lunch, dinner with Sally and some others. The villagers like to share meals. Here it's not polite to eat by yourself all the time. We often have guests over to eat with us, or go to a neighbour's house.

Art doesn't miss Mum and Dad. He eats, drinks, plays and behaves the same as always. Doesn't cry when Sally gives him a bath. He does give her a sharp nip on her left forearm at one stage, leaving deep marks, but that's normal for Art.

"We should stitch his lips together when he's not eating," Sally says, rubbing her arm. But she's only joking. Sally loves kids. Of course, she'd rather not be bitten, but the whole village knows about Art's biting habits. Sally knew what she was letting herself in for when she offered to have us.

It's strange not having Mum and Dad around. Things were different when we lived in the city. They often went out at night, leaving me with a babysitter. And they'd go for holidays by themselves occasionally. I didn't mind. I enjoyed staying with other people — I always got loads of treats.

But for the last year we've been together all the time. I've got used to them being at home every night. I feel like I did when I lost my favourite teddy bear a few years ago. It was a scruffy grey bear, nothing special, but I'd had it since I was a baby. It had been my constant companion, even when I'd outgrown my other teddies. I took it to bed, on holiday, even to the cinema. I felt like a friend had died when I lost it.

This is almost the same. Not as bad because I know Mum and Dad will come back. But strange. Like something's wrong with the world.

→I'm uneasy when it's time for bed. Sally's spare bed is soft, but it smells damp, like my socks when they're wet. Art goes to sleep immediately, delighted to be sharing a bed with me. But I can't drop off. I'm tired – I woke early, knowing Mum and Dad were leaving – but my eyelids won't stay closed.

I think about Mrs Egin. I haven't seen her since that morning when she witched out on me. I've taken the long way to school and back every day since. I've tried to laugh it off, make like it was no big deal. Told myself I imagined the curses and her stroking the patch of light.

But I know what I saw. I can't pretend it didn't happen. And although I'm not as scared as I was that first night, I'm still shaken, afraid to close my eyes in case she's there when I open them, standing over me, cackling, a knife to my throat.

I turn from my left side to my right, then back again. I try lying flat on my back, then on my stomach. Nothing works.

Annoyed, I stop trying to sleep, hoping I'll drift off by accident. I look round the small, cosy room, then focus on the patches of light. They look the same as ever, various shapes and shades. I count triangles, quadrangles, pentagons, sextants... No, that's an instrument. Sextuplet? I'm not sure. I think that's right, but I'm not... maybe it's a...

→I wake suddenly. *Hexagon!* Of course. Can't believe I had trouble remembering that. The brain can play funny tricks when you're tired. I turn, yawning, looking for Art.

He isn't there.

At first, I think he's just slipped further down beneath the covers, but when I lift them there's no sign of him.

I sit up swiftly, sensing danger, recalling Mum's last words to me — "Look after your brother." Flash on an image of Mrs Egin sneaking in, stealing Art, putting him in a big black pot and boiling him alive.

My world is never truly dark. The patches of light mean I can see pretty well even on the blackest night. Mum and Dad used to try to convince me that the lights weren't real, but if they're imaginary, why do I have such fantastic night vision?

I get out of bed and hurry to the door, so certain Art isn't in the room that my gaze glides right over him and I almost crash into him. Then my senses click in and I stop. Blink a couple of times to properly clear my eyes.

Art's in the middle of the room. There's a large patch of orange light pulsing just over his head. He's playing with marbles which Sally gave to me earlier. He's holding two of them up over his eyes. They're orange-coloured, like the light.

Art sees me and smiles, looking at me through the orange marbles. For a brief second I'm positive that somebody or something is in the room with us. I think I hear a soft growling noise. My head snaps left, then right — nothing. I look back at Art. In the strange orange light, with the marbles covering his eyes, he doesn't look like my brother. I start to think that it's not Art, that he's been replaced by some evil spirit, that the witch *has* been here. I feel afraid. I back up to the bed.

"Art?" I say, very softly. "Is that you? Are you OK?"

A giggle breaks the spell. Art lowers the marbles. And I see that of course it's him.

"Idiot!" I laugh weakly at myself. I go pick Art up and take the marbles away. Sally said not to let him have them in case he swallowed one. Art grumbles and tries to grab them back, but I tell him they're dangerous. He understands that and snuggles into me, nuzzling my shoulder with his teeth, but gently, not like when he bites somebody.

I stand there with Art, feeling cold but happy, smiling at how silly I was. Art falls asleep in my arms. I carry him back to bed, tuck him in, then climb in beside him. Lying on my side, I stare at the orange light, still pulsing. It seems to have grown bigger, but that's not unusual — the patches often change size.

I don't like this orange light. There's something creepy about it. It reminds me of the pink light which Mrs Egin stroked. I turn my back on it and shut my eyes tight, trying to fall asleep again. But I can still sense it there, hanging in the cold night air, lighting up the room with its ominous orange glow. Pulsing.

DING DONG

→Two days later. The orange light is still pulsing and changing size. Although I can call it closer like the other patches, I can't send it away more than twenty or twenty-five feet. It's started to bug me, like an insect which keeps buzzing in front of my face. An uneasiness chews away at me every time I catch sight of it. I know it's crazy, worrying about a light, but I can't help myself. I have a bad feeling about this.

→It's a lovely sunny day. Our teacher, Logan Rile, decided not to waste the weather, so we're having lessons outside, in one of the fields around Paskinston. There are thirty-four of us, a variety of classes and ages, sitting in a semi-circle around Logan. He's telling us about tectonic plates. Logan's not the best teacher. He sometimes forgets he's talking to children and gets too technical. Very few of us understand everything he says. But he's interesting, and the bits that make sense are fascinating. It's also fun when you *do* understand him — it makes you feel clever.

Some of the younger children from the crèche have come with us. Their normal minder has gone to the fair and her replacement's finding it hard to cope with so many little ones. She was delighted when Logan offered to take a few off her hands for the day.

Art's playing with the orange marbles beside me. I shouldn't let him have them, but he really likes them. Anyway, he hasn't put them in his mouth yet. I keep a close eye on him, checking every couple of minutes to make sure both marbles are in sight — not in his stomach.

"So these plates are moving all the time?" Bryan Colbert asks. Bryan's one of the eldest children, nearly seventeen.

"Yes," Logan says.

"Then why don't countries move?"

"They do," Logan says. "The continents are drifting all the time. It's very slow, but it's happening. One day Australia will collide with America or Africa – I can never remember which – and the effects will be catastrophic. New mountains will be thrust upwards. There'll be tidal waves. Dust will clog the air. Billions of people and animals will die. It might be the end of all life on this planet."

"*All* life?" Dave English – a kid a year younger than me – asks.

"Yes."

"But I didn't think that could happen. Everybody… everything… can't just die. Won't God keep some of us alive?"

"No god can prevent the end of life on this planet," Logan says in his usual serious way. "Or the end of life in this universe. Everything has an end. That's the way life is. But maybe there'll be a new beginning when our world ends. New life, new creatures, new means of existence."

"That's scary," Dave mutters. "I don't want everything to die."

"Nor me," Logan smiles. "But our wants are irrelevant. This is the way things are. We can accept the truth and deal with it, or live in ignorance. Death is nothing to be afraid of. Once you think it through and get it into perspective, it's not so bad. In fact, many people—"

"*Now!*" a woman screams, cutting Logan off. All our heads turn at once, as if our necks were connected. I see Mrs Egin lumbering up behind us, fingers twitching, frothing at the mouth. "Now it happens! Up the throat, past the gums, look out world, here it comes!"

The pink light which I saw her stroking a few days ago has grown much bigger and now seems to be touching her just behind her head. It's pulsing quickly. Other patches of light around it are pulsing too, and moving towards it, as though magnetically drawn to it.

"Mrs Egin?" Logan says, rising, signalling for the rest of us to stay seated. "Are you all right?"

"They said I couldn't do it! Thought I wasn't strong enough to summon them!" She laughs her witch's laugh, then sings, "Wrong! Wrong! Wrong! Now! Now! Now!"

"Mrs Egin, I think you should—"

"You will see me die!" she shouts and her eyes scan the group, fixing on me. "Find the thief! Who's the thief? Find him!"

Fear comes shooting back. I'm not as afraid as when I was alone with her, but I'm pretty petrified. The others are too. We huddle close together, shuffling into a tighter group for protection.

Logan steps forward. "Let me take you home, Mrs Egin. We'll get you to bed, I'll call for a doctor, and you'll be right as rain in—"

Mrs Egin roars a word I don't know. Her lips are moving fast now, in that strange language she was speaking before. Logan stops short and hesitates. That scares me even more — it's bad news when your teacher is as frightened as you are.

The pulsing patches of light are moving faster, drawn towards the pink light. They merge with it, then flow into Mrs Egin. Now she's glowing from within, the lights beneath her flesh, spreading through her body.

I stumble to my feet. "The lights!" I gasp.

Logan looks back at me. "Calm down, Kernel."

"But the lights! Can't you see them?"

"What lights?"

"Inside her! She's swallowing the lights!"

Mrs Egin cackles while Logan stares at me dumbly. I glance around. Everyone's looking at me oddly. They can't see the lights. There's nothing any of them can do to stop this happening.

I focus on Mrs Egin. A bulging, pulsing bubble of light has formed behind and above her, patches melting together, colours mixing, flowing into her. Her eyes are bowls of light. I can't see her lips — multicoloured froth hides them. Her skin appears to be rippling.

"Mrs Egin," Logan tries again, facing her. "You have to–"

The witch shrieks triumphantly. A piercing note of wickedness and victory. I cover my ears with my hands. Logan covers his too. My eyes scrunch shut, but I quickly force them open a crack. I see Mrs Egin stagger backwards. She goes stiff, arms wide at her sides, head cocked to the left. A gentle, tender smile crosses her lips.

Then the lights explode through her. And *she* explodes. Scraps fly everywhere — flesh, bone, guts, blood. Logan and the kids at the front are splattered by the spray. They squeal with disgust and terror. A chunk of bone hits Logan hard in the face and he drops, grunting with pain.

I cover my eyes and drag Art in close, turning him away from the carnage. I'm screaming. Everybody is. But I can still hear Mrs Egin's scream over the sound of all the others, even though she can't be making any noise now.

For an uncountable number of seconds the witch's scream holds, mingling with ours. Then it stops. All the screaming stops in the space of a second or two. Eerie, unnatural silence.

I don't want to take my arm away, but I must. I have to look. Others are peeping too, although most are still covering their eyes or looking away from where the witch was standing.

Mrs Egin is gone. Nothing of her remains, except a circle of blood and grisly carnage, covering the grass, Logan and many of the children. And at the centre of the circle — a panel of greyness.

The large grey patch of light hangs motionless a foot or two above the ground. It's three or four feet wide, maybe six or seven high. Jagged round the edges.

I'm not the only one who can see this light. Others are pointing at it, gasping, murmuring, "What the hell is that?" This is a different type of light from the ones I usually see.

Logan rises, rubbing his head. Stares in disbelief at the gory mess, then at the grey wall of light. He's an educated, experienced man. But he's seen nothing like this before.

"She exploded!" a boy yells, excited. "Did you see her? It was amazing!"

"Is she dead?" a girl asks, voice trembling.

"What's that light?"

"Yeah, what is it?"

"Yeah."

Logan walks round the panel of light. I can only see his feet when he's behind it. Then he comes back into view. He's more bewildered than afraid, like most of the kids around me. The light has made more of an impression than Mrs Egin exploding! Perhaps they're in shock, not ready to deal with the explosion — and her death — yet.

"We have to get away from here."

I hadn't meant to speak, but now that the words have popped out, I know I'm right. Everybody gawps at me. "This is bad!" I shout. "That light's dangerous. We have to run."

"It's OK, Kernel," Logan says. "This is mind-blowing, but we're in the midst of something wondrous. I'm not sure what's going on, but this is a once in a lifetime opportunity to experience the miraculous. Mrs Egin... this light... it's incredible!" He beams with delight.

Some kids get to their feet and drift towards Logan and the panel of grey light. They're not afraid now that Logan isn't. They trust him. They think he knows best.

"This is wrong!" I yell. "It's evil! Can't you feel it?"

"You shouldn't be so suspicious, Kernel," Logan laughs uneasily.

"You're covered in blood!" I roar angrily, unable to believe that someone so smart can be this stupid. "Mrs Egin's dead! You're walking through her guts!"

Logan blinks. Looks down at his blood-soaked shirt and trousers. His red hands. The mess around him. "Oh," he says quietly. "Oh my—"

Something bursts out of the grey light. It has two long legs, a stumpy, leathery body, four arms which end in thick, hairy fingers. A dark green head, a cross between a human's and a dog's. No mouth. Long draping ears. Wide, white, evil eyes.

The thing grabs Logan. It somehow makes a hissing, whistling noise. Logan stares at it in shock. Two of its hands lock on his head. The others clasp his shoulders. The hairs on its fingers extend, growing at an unnatural speed, digging into the flesh of Logan's face. One hair darts into his right eye, puncturing it. Logan shrieks with pain.

Then the thing's upper arms jerk apart quickly — ripping Logan's head off his neck! The monster tosses it to the ground. Stamps down hard with its right foot. And Logan's severed head pops like a melon dropped from a great height.

The thing looks at the rest of us. Spreads its arms and hisses. And thirty-four kids scream as one and crap their pants.

KIDNAP

→Chaos. Everyone's running, crashing into each other, falling, screaming. I'm part of the madness. Clutching Art in my arms. Fleeing blindly. Away from the grey light and the four-armed monster. Trying to stay on my feet. Weeping, partly because Logan has been killed, mostly because I'm terrified.

A girl smashes into me and knocks me to the ground. I manage to fall with Art on top of me, so he isn't injured. He's laughing — he thinks this is a game. I start to yell at the girl, but then I see blood gushing from her throat, her arms thrashing. She topples over. Flops about, then goes very still.

I look away before I can focus on her face. I don't want to know who she is. Right now I want to concentrate on the one thing that matters more than anything else — getting out of here before the monster kills me.

I push myself to my feet, chest heaving. Look for the best way out. It's hard to tell. I'm surrounded on all sides by panic. I count two, three, four dead children — then stop. I don't want to know the numbers.

The monster's on top of a boy — Dave English, who was so afraid of death. The beast's fingers are buried in Dave's stomach. It's gazing around, white eyes darting from one child to another. Like it's choosing its next victim. Or looking for someone in particular.

I'm getting ready to run again when I spot movement in the panel of grey light. A man steps through. Behind him is a blonde woman. Another woman after her, Indian, wearing a sari. Then a second dark-skinned man.

The Indian woman curses when she sees the corpses. Starts after the monster, her hands coming up, murder in her eyes.

"Sharmila! No!" barks the first man. He's old. He has a short beard and messy dark hair. A shabby suit.

"We must stop this!" the Indian woman shouts.

"No," the man repeats, and I can tell by his tone that he's accustomed to being obeyed.

"Master..." the second man says uncertainly. He has the darkest skin I've ever seen, as if his mother was the night.

"I know, Raz," the first man snaps. "But we mustn't kill him."

"The children," the Indian woman snarls. "I will not stand by and let that demon murder all these children. That would be monstrous."

"She is right, master," the black man says.

"Oh, very well," the man in the shabby suit grumbles. "We'll save as many of the young as we can. We don't want to be considered barbarians." He laughs then signals for the others to spread out. "Work Cadaver back to the window and force him through. We'll track him down again later."

This sudden appearance and surreal conversation has astonished me so much, I'm standing still instead of fleeing for safety. The monster – a *demon*, the woman said – has moved on from Dave English and is lolloping after a girl. She's racing from it like an Olympic sprinter, but the monster's legs are longer and it catches up with her in a couple of seconds. Reaches out with its long, hairy fingers… then recoils when the ground at its feet explodes upwards.

The demon makes a high whistling sound, its head snapping round. It spots the four humans who came through the panel (or window, as the man called it). It glares at them, white eyes filled with fury and hate. They're closing in on it from both sides, leaving a path to the window free. Pale blue light crackles from the black man's fingertips — I guess he made the ground explode, distracting the monster and saving the girl.

Art bites my right arm, hard. It's the first time he's ever bitten me. I get such a shock, I drop him and collapse on my bum. He lands with a heavy thud, rolls over, then crawls towards the demon, gurgling happily. He must think it's some giant toy. He's so anxious to play with it, he bit me so I'd release him.

"Art!" I yell. "Come back! It's…"

The demon spots me. Its white eyes roll down and fix on Art. It gives a loud, high-pitched whistle. And then it's running towards us, impossibly long steps. I barely have time to register fear — then it's on us. It stoops, picks Art up with one hand, hisses like a nest of snakes.

"*No!*" I cry, leaping at the demon, forgetting my fear, caring only about Art. I land on the monster's left side. From a distance I thought its skin was leathery, but now I realise it's more like an insect's brittle shell. My fists crunch into it, knocking crinkly flakes loose. I'm yelling wildly, the way I always do when I get into a fight.

I tug at its hairy arms — they feel like strands of seaweed — desperately reaching for Art. The demon hisses again then knocks me aside. I land hard on my right arm. It twists beneath me and snaps. I roar with pain, but roll over and force myself back to my feet, woozy but determined to rescue Art.

But the demon isn't there. It's racing towards the grey window, Art cradled in its arms, head down, legs a whirl of motion.

"Beranabus!" the Indian woman shouts.

"Let him go," the leader of the quartet says.

"But the child…"

"Not our problem."

"*Art!*" I bellow, tears streaming from my eyes. It's hopeless, but I run after the demon, praying for the strength and speed to draw level with it before it reaches the window.

The demon pauses at the panel of grey light. Looks back at the four adults. It hisses and shakes Art at them, mocking them. The hairs of its hands wrap round Art's ankles then snake up his legs. He's giggling, tugging at the monster's floppy ears, no idea of the danger he's in. He drops his orange marbles — he's found something better to play with.

The Indian woman snarls and extends a hand towards the demon. She starts muttering the words of what sounds like a spell. Before she can complete it, the monster jumps at the window, hits the grey light and vanishes. Returns to whatever hellish place it came from — with Art.

→I sink to my knees, stunned, staring at the window. Around me — screams, sobbing, moans. The stench of blood and death. Calls from the village as terrified adults race towards their stricken children, too late to help, only in time to mop up the blood.

The four people who came through after the monster have gathered by the window. The light is pulsing again. The edges are throbbing inwards, turning white. The leader stands in front of the panel.

"Do you think he's waiting for us on the other side?" the dark-skinned man asks.

The leader shrugs. "Only one way to find out." He steps forward and disappears like the demon. The blonde woman follows, then the black man. The Indian woman pauses and looks round the field of misery. Her gaze rests on me. She winces. Starts to say something. Changes her mind and steps into the light.

→I'm dazed. Shaking from shock and the pain in my right arm. Silently staring at the grey light as it pulses quicker and quicker, the edges closing in. It's about to collapse, break apart, become fragmented patches of light again.

Fresh screams as parents find the remains of their children. A chorus of wails, growing by the second, becoming a wall of anguished sound. Some kids are still running. They don't know it's finished, that the monster's gone, that the last victim was Art.

I stumble towards the flickering window, wanting to believe there's hope, that the Indian woman will reappear with Art in her arms. Art can't be gone for ever. I can't have lost him. He's my brother.

I spot the marbles on the ground by the window. I pick them up, study their orange centres, then put them in my left trouser pocket. I'm numb. Hardly aware of the throbbing pain in my broken arm.

I think about Mum and Dad, how they'll react when they return to find Paskinston in mourning, Art abducted. Mum's last words to me echo inside my skull — "Look after your brother." Dad calling me the best brother in the world, saying I'd take better care of Art than they could.

But I didn't. I let a demon take him.

Staring into the heart of the grey light. I tune out the screams. Focus on the window. A voice whispers to me, a voice I haven't heard for a year. Tells me what I must do. What it suggests is crazy. I should dismiss it immediately. But I can't.

The window is closing. Any second now, it'll be gone. But if I step forward before it closes... chase after the demon... perhaps I can find Art, rescue him, bring him back home.

Madness. Art's probably dead already, slaughtered by the demon as soon as it escaped. Besides, I don't know what lies on the other side of the window. Most likely more monsters like the one that took Art. I'll almost certainly be killed. Even if I'm not, there'll be no way back once the window breaks up. Mum and Dad will lose both their children. Double the sorrow. I should forget about it. Ignore the voice and its suicidal suggestion.

But I can't. Because they'll blame me. They won't want to, but the accusation will be there, in their eyes. A look that says, "You didn't take care of him. He was your brother. You didn't protect him. You let him go. It's your fault."

The edges of the window bend inward. The grey light sputters. There's no more time. I have to decide.

I start to look back, wanting the window to close before I can act, to cheat myself of the chance to go after

Art. But as my head turns, my feet move forward. Instinct makes me step through the grey light of the window — into the realm of the murderous demon.

WALKING ON WATER

→The greyness lasts a few seconds. Like a mist around me, except there's no damp or cool sensation. Then it parts and I find myself surrounded by trees. A forest of crooked, twisted, pitiful trees.

They're howling.

At first I think something else is making the horrible noise, like a mix of car brakes squealing and somebody sawing through metal. My brain tells me there are workmen nearby, or a weird animal. But then I see the trees moving, swaying weakly. There are holes in their dark, mottled bark. And the howls are coming from the holes. No question about it.

I try applying logic to the situation, like Mr Spock. The howls must be the wind blowing through the holes. Except there isn't any wind. And I know – I *know* – that the trees are making the noise themselves. They're alive. In pain. Howling with anger, hatred — and hunger.

I look for the window but there's nothing. Either you can't see it from this side or it broke up into pieces while I was staring at the trees.

I take a hesitant step forward. There's a soft splashing sound. I look down. See water everywhere underfoot, covering the ground. I look again at the trees. I can't see any roots. They're all below the waterline.

I crouch, trying to see how deep the water is. But it's murky and muddy, and the trees block out most of the light. I stick a finger in. It slides down to the first knuckle, the second, the beginning of my palm. I push my hand in up to my wrist without touching anything solid. Stare at my hand, then my feet. I *could* be standing on a platform. Except I know – the same way I knew about the trees – that I'm not.

I'm standing on the surface of the water!

I rise quickly, fear setting in again, certain I'm about to drop and drown. But although water splashes when I move my feet, I don't sink. I explore with my right foot, angling it downwards. It dips into the water. But when I bring it back up, level my foot and plant my sole down, the surface supports me.

I take one step. Two. A third. It's not the same as walking on land. More like walking across the floor of an inflatable castle. But somehow, impossibly, the water keeps me up.

I smile at the craziness of it, then gasp as pain flares in my right arm. I'd completely forgotten about my broken limb. The sudden surge of pain reminds me that I'm walking wounded. I've never broken an arm before. It doesn't hurt as much as I thought it would, but it's certainly no picnic.

I carry on walking, trying to keep my arm from jolting. Easier said than done — the watery floor is uneven, hard to balance on. I don't feel as if I'm going to fall, but I tilt left and right quite often. I have to use my arms to maintain my balance, which sets off the pain again.

I deliberately don't think about where I am or the impossibility of walking on water. I can't care about stuff like that. I'm here to find Art. Nothing else matters. I can marvel at the rest of it once we're both back home, safe with Sally.

Yeah, like that's gonna happen, an inner voice sniggers.

I ignore it. Try not to let the howls of the trees unsettle me. Stagger on in search of my kidnapped brother.

→The water has seeped through my shoes and socks, and is climbing up the legs of my trousers. I take no notice. I have bigger things to worry about.

There's no sign of the four humans, the demon or Art. And no way of tracking them. If we were in a normal forest, perhaps there would be footprints. But apart from ripples as I move across the water, the surface is smooth, unmarked.

I haven't seen any animals or birds. Only the trees. And there aren't even leaves on those. I'd think they were dead if not for the howls, which echo relentlessly. The noise is like needles poking away at my eardrums.

What now? the voice inside my head asks.

"Keep walking," I answer aloud, trying to drown out the howls of the trees. "They have to be here somewhere. I'll find them."

Not necessarily. They might have gone through another window. Or maybe they didn't come out the same place you did.

"I'll find them," I insist.

What if you don't? There's nothing to eat. Nowhere to aim for — every bit of this forest looks the same. And how will you sleep? The water might not hold you if you lie down. Even if it does, it'll drench you to the bone.

"I can sleep on the branches of a tree."

Maybe they eat humans, the voice suggests.

"Don't be stupid," I mutter unconvincingly. "And there are probably fish in the water. I can catch one to eat."

Or it might catch you, the voice notes. *There could be sharks. Underwater monsters. Waiting. Moving in for the kill. Underneath you right this min—*

"Shut up," I growl.

→"Art!" I yell. "Art!"

No answer. The screech of the trees would probably muffle his cry even if he was here and trying to call back. It's hopeless. I'll never find him. He's probably dead anyway, ripped to pieces by the demon. I should try to find a way home. Worry about myself, not my doomed brother.

But I can't think that way. I won't. I've got to believe he's alive. The thought of returning home without Art (even if I knew how) is too awful to consider.

I've no idea how long I've been here. My watch isn't working — it stopped when I came through the grey window. Feels like a few hours. I'm wet, cold, miserable, alone. Trying hard not to think about Logan and the kids killed by the demon. Flinching every time my brain recycles an image of the bloodshed. I force myself to focus on other memories. There's no time to deal with the massacre. I have to concentrate on finding Art.

Some small orange patches of light are flashing several feet ahead of me. They began pulsing soon after I got here. They move with me as I wander the watery forest, keeping me company.

I come to a semi-clearing. The trees don't grow so thickly together here. I can see the sky, gloomy and purplish. The sun shines dimly on my left-hand side — and a second sun shines weakly to my right!

I rub my eyes and look again. The suns are still there. Not strong like the sun I'm used to. Smaller, duller. I'm not as amazed by the twin suns as I should be — the water and howling trees tipped me off to the fact that I wasn't on my own world any more. I wonder how day and night work here, or if there even is a night.

As I'm staring upwards, several patches of pulsing light pass by. Different colours, shapes and sizes, slowly gliding along in the same direction. I look around and notice other patches floating through the trees, converging on a point far off to my left. Without any kind of trail, I've been walking aimlessly. Now I decide to follow the moving lights.

→Maybe an hour later I spot the four humans who came through the window after the demon. They're standing in a clearing, the old bearded man slightly apart from the others. I think he's muttering a spell, hands wriggling by his sides. He's the focus for the moving, pulsing lights. They're gathering in the space in front of him, slotting together, forming a window like the one in the village field.

I creep up without them seeing me.

"...still say we should have killed him," the Indian woman is saying. "It was not right, letting him murder the children and take one of them. We are supposed to protect people. That is our duty."

"The master knows what he is doing," the black man says. "He would not have let the demon go without good cause."

"You'll get used to people dying," the young blonde woman says. "Beranabus isn't interested in saving the lives of a few individuals. He doesn't have time for trivialities."

"*Trivialities?*" the Indian woman explodes. "You call the loss of human life a trivi–"

"No," the younger woman interrupts. "That's what Beranabus calls it. He says we serve a greater purpose, that our mission is nothing less than the protection of mankind itself. He says we can't worry about every human killed by demons, or waste time chasing strays. He doesn't mind you lot doing it, but we—"

"I'm trying to work!" the elderly man — Beranabus — barks, turning angrily. "If you'd stop chattering like monkeys, maybe I could…" He sees me and stops. "Who the hell is that?"

The others whirl around defensively. They pause when they see me.

"He doesn't look like a demon," the black man says.

"Some don't," the young woman growls. "A few can take human form. You have to be careful." She raises her right hand. I sense power in her fingertips. Power directed at *me*.

"No!" I cry. "Don't hurt me! I'm not a demon! I'm Kernel Fleck!"

The young woman's fingers curl inward, holding back the magical power which she was about to unleash. She frowns. "He doesn't sound like a demon."

"It is the boy from the village," the Indian woman says. "He was with the child Cadaver kidnapped." She smiles at me. "Hello."

"Hi," I squeak nervously.

"What's he doing here?" Beranabus huffs.

"I imagine he came through the window after us," the Indian woman says. "In search of his brother perhaps?" She arches an eyebrow questioningly at me.

"Yes. The monster — demon — stole my brother, Art. I came to get him back."

"Nonsense," Beranabus snorts. "It will have slaughtered and devoured him by now."

"Beranabus!" the Indian woman hisses. "Do not say such a thing!"

"Why not? It's true."

"You do not know that. And even if it is, you should not say it. Not in front of…" She nods at me.

Beranabus laughs. "If the child was bold enough to follow us, he's bold enough to be told the truth. Isn't that right, boy? We don't have to lie. You'd rather we were honest about it, aye?"

"Art isn't dead," I say, my voice trembling. "He's alive. I'm going to get him back."

"Steal him back from Cadaver?" Beranabus laughs again. "You're brave, but stupid. You couldn't find him, not if you searched for the rest of your life. So it doesn't really matter if he's alive or not, does it?"

"Is that the demon's name?" I ask, ignoring his question. "Cadaver?"

"Aye. But that's no use to you. What are you going to do — report him to your police?"

"We have to send this boy back," the young woman says. "Open another window. Return him."

"We don't have time," Beranabus says. "Cadaver knows we're after him. He's on the run. The further ahead he gets, the harder he'll be to find."

"That doesn't matter. We must—"

"You're chasing him?" I cut in, excited. "You're going after the monster who stole my brother?"

"Aye," Beranabus says, eyes twinkling.

"Then I'll come with you. Please. Let me. When you find him, if Art's still... you know... I can snatch him back. Take him home."

"No," the Indian woman says immediately. "It is too dangerous. You do not know what you would be letting yourself in for... Excuse me, but what did you say your name was?"

"Kernel. Kernel Fleck."

"My name is Sharmila." She smiles. "You must go home, Kernel. If we find your brother, we will return him to you. I promise."

"No," I say stubbornly. "I want to help find him."

"*Help?*" Beranabus repeats, cocking an amused eyebrow. "How exactly do you plan to *help?*"

"I... I don't know. With the spells? The lights?"

"What lights?" Beranabus frowns.

I point to the patches of light which are joining together ahead of him. He looks at where I'm pointing and his frown deepens. I realise these people can't see the patches either. Before I can explain, the black man speaks up.

"Sharmila and Nadia are right, master. This child does not belong here. We must return him. If we don't... if we leave him in this nightmarish world of water and screaming trees... we will be no better than the demons we seek to stop."

Beranabus sniffs. "A nice plea, Raz, but I never claimed to be any better than the Demonata. I say we leave him, and my word is final — isn't it, Nadia?"

He looks hard at the young woman. She stares back defiantly for a few seconds, then drops her gaze. "It wouldn't take long to open a window..." she mutters. "I could do it while you search for Cadaver."

"You're not very skilled at finding your way around," Beranabus says. "What makes you think you could locate the right place?"

"I could try," she insists. "And even if I don't find the exact spot, I can return him to our world. He could make his own way home from there."

Beranabus thinks a moment, then shrugs. "So be it. Waste your time if you wish. But keep out of my way, so you don't interfere with–"

"I'm not going!" I shout. "I came to find Art and I'm not going home without him!"

"Kernel," the black man – Raz – says, "you don't know what is happening. This is not a place for children. You must go home. Mustn't he, Sharmila?"

"Yes," the Indian woman says, glaring at me like an angry teacher. "I gave you my word that I will return your brother to you if we find him alive. That will have to be enough."

"Trust me," the younger woman — Nadia — says with a sad smile, "you don't want to stay here. You've followed us into a different universe — the home of the Demonata. It's a hell-hole. This part isn't so bad, but we're going to encounter far worse very soon. You don't want to be with us when that happens. *I* wouldn't be here if I had a choice."

"I don't care," I say, close to tears. "Art's my brother. Mum told me to look after him. I'm not going back alone." Softly, voice cracking, I add, "I can't."

Sharmila's eyes go soft with pity. "I am sorry, Kernel. We have spoken harshly. But you have to understand — it is impossible. You cannot stay. You could do no good here. You must go home. Your parents will be frantic, thinking they have lost you both. That is not fair, is it?"

"No, but…" I can't find the words to explain.

"Enough talk," Beranabus grunts, losing his patience. "The boy wants to stay… you lot want to send him home… this is easily decided."

He flicks a hand at me. Suddenly, I'm flying through the air. I smack hard into a tree and cry out with shock and pain, mostly from my broken arm. As I fall to the ground, the branches of the tree move quickly. Catch me. Wrap themselves round me. Squeeze.

I catch sight of Sharmila darting to my rescue. Beranabus waves a hand, stopping her. The branches tighten. The tree howls louder than ever. I'm lifted up. The holes in its bark are expanding. It means to crush and swallow me. A few seconds more and I'll be dead, killed and eaten by this monstrous sham of a tree.

Something flares within me. I scream at the tree, set my teeth on the nearest branch to my face and bite hard. The tree screeches. I chew through the branch, snapping it loose. Another. My left arm comes free. There's heat in my palm. I grab a branch and feel power shoot through my hand, into the wood.

The tree howls with pain, then abruptly releases me. I drop, hit the water, go under, come up spluttering and thrashing. I dip under again. This time I stay there, feeling the water drag me down. I realise the water's alive too, like the trees. Just as hungry and eager to kill.

I fight the panic. Force my legs to stop kicking wildly. Direct the power in my palm down towards my feet. I imagine myself as a rocket, blasting off, breaking free of the pull of the water. For a few seconds nothing happens. My lungs tighten. My mouth twitches.

Then, in a sudden burst, I explode upwards, out of the water, coughing, shivering, but free. I land on my feet and this time the surface of the water holds. There's terrible pain in my broken arm as I land, but I quickly use the power to numb myself to it.

I face Beranabus, furious at him for launching me at the tree and nearly killing me. Ready to attack him, to use my power to smash him to pieces.

He's laughing. The others are staring at me, stunned, but Beranabus is laughing. "I thought so!" he cackles. "I guessed there was more to this one than mere flesh and bone. Ordinary children don't step out of their own world into the universe of the Demonata. You need to be one of us to be that crazy. We'll hold on to him."

"No!" Sharmila cries.

"But... master... he's only a child," Raz mumbles.

"This is a bad idea," Nadia adds.

"I don't care," Beranabus says, waving away their protests. He grins at me, but it's the smile of a cut-throat pirate. "You want to stay and help us find Cadaver? You want to search for your brother and rescue him like a knight of old? Very well, boy, you've got your wish." He sticks out an arm, even though we're too far from each other to shake hands. "You're one of us now, Kernel Fleck. A demon hunter. Welcome to the Disciples!"

DEMONS AND DISCIPLES

→Beranabus is still working on his spells. Trying to find Cadaver and open a window which will lead us to the creature. According to Nadia there are thousands of demon worlds like this. Cadaver could be on almost any of them.

I'm squatting with the Disciples in a semi-circle. We can't sit down because of the water. They look tired and upset. Sharmila argued with Beranabus for a long time, insisting he send me back. She said he was irresponsible and vile. He just swore and told her not to tell him his business. He said when she'd lived as long as he had, and seen all the things he'd seen, she could lecture him — but only then.

I study the Disciples while Beranabus works. Sharmila's the eldest, fifty or more (though I'm not very good at guessing ages). She has a painted red spot in the middle of her forehead. I should know the name for it, but I can't remember. Wrinkly skin. Dark, soft eyes. A long sari, many colours, ripped in several places and stained round the edges with blood and dirt.

Raz is fat and black. His skin's incredibly dark. If it was night, no moon and he shut his eyes, he'd be invisible. Tight, curly hair. Not overly tall. Maybe in his thirties. He wears a very fine suit. I think he's wealthy — he looks like someone who hasn't worked with his hands a lot. No shoes — none of the Disciples wears shoes or socks.

Nadia is in her late teens or early twenties. She has short blonde hair, blue eyes and very bad skin. Lots of spots and acne scars. A hard, plain face. She wouldn't be especially pretty even if she had the clearest skin in the world. Plump, but with bony legs and arms. She wears jeans and a dark green jumper. Looks unhappy, as though she's suffered a lot.

Nadia catches me watching her and smiles. Her whole face changes. She looks a lot prettier. "Strange days, huh, Kernel Fleck?"

"I still don't understand it all," I mutter. "Actually, I don't really understand any of it."

Nadia laughs. "At least you're honest." She chews a fingernail, considering what to say. Eventually, she gestures at the elderly man on his feet. "That's Beranabus. He's a magician. There aren't many of them in the world. Lots of people can do some magic if the situation is right, but only a few are born with full magical powers."

"He is our master," Raz says, gazing at Beranabus adoringly. "He unites us, gives us direction, shows us the way."

"He is an egotistical, reckless fool!" Sharmila disagrees, snorting harshly. "He cares nothing for any person's life. He claims to be on a greater mission to save the world, but I have my doubts. I do not trust him and I advise you to be cautious also, Kernel."

"But isn't he your leader?" I ask, confused.

"Yes. But we follow him reluctantly, not out of choice." She looks at Raz and smiles. "Well, some of us do."

Raz and Sharmila start arguing about Beranabus's faults and strong points. Nadia listens for a while, then shuffles away from them and nods for me to follow.

"They're new to this," she says quietly when we're out of earshot. "Beranabus has always been a legendary figure to them. They haven't spent time around him, so they're not sure how to respond to his... peculiarities. Raz over-idolises him. Sharmila criticises. But he doesn't care what people say or think, as long as they obey his orders."

"You've been with him a long time?" I ask and she nods. "Is he your father or something?"

Nadia laughs. "No, he's just..." She pauses and chews another fingernail. "We've all been where you are now. Sharmila, Raz and I led normal lives once. We sensed we were different, not completely like other people. But we had families and friends, jobs and dreams. We were ordinary. Happy. Then, one way or another, we found out about the Demonata."

"The demons?"

"Yes. That's their proper name — Demonata. They exist in a multi-world universe of their own. They've been around as long as mankind, maybe longer. Evil, murderous creatures, who revel in torment and slaughter. They try to cross over into our world all the time, but most are either too weak or too strong."

"Too strong?" I frown.

"You stepped through a window to get here," she explains. "Windows are the most common way of moving between universes, but they're limited in size. Larger, stronger demons can't squeeze through. There are other ways to cross — tunnels can be created — but they're rare.

"Anyway, demons are real and they like nothing better than to cross into our world and murder humans. They're usually unable to stay in our universe more than a few minutes, so they only have time to kill a handful of people. They've slaughtered hundreds of thousands over the centuries, but for the most part we've escaped pretty lightly, protected by the laws of physics."

Nadia glances at Beranabus, still working to find Cadaver. The patches of light have stopped gliding towards him, but there are lots in the air around the magician, pulsing at different speeds. As he chants spells, pieces slot together, joining in a panel forming in front of him. It's strange that only I can see the lights, but I don't comment on that in case I break Nadia's train of thought.

"Centuries ago, a few mages – people with magical talents, but not true magicians – decided to actively combat the demons," Nadia continues. "They studied the disturbances created in advance of a demon crossing to our universe. If they could predict their coming, they could stop the beasts or fight them when they entered our world. They recruited other mages, then approached Beranabus and tried–"

"Wait a minute," I interrupt. "You said this happened hundreds of years ago."

"Yes."

"But…" I stare at the elderly, bearded magician. He looks maybe sixty or more, but nothing like a guy in his hundreds, assuming a man could live that long — which is impossible.

"Time works differently in the Demonata's universe," Nadia says. "It can move more slowly or quickly, depending on where you are. But normally it's slower. An hour here could be a day or more on Earth. A week could be a year. You could spend three or four years here and return to a brand new century. Or spend ten years here and return to a world which has only moved on by a week.

"But humans can't survive in this universe. Even real magicians fall foul of the demon forces. Several have tried to extend their natural lifespan by coming here, but they've all been ripped to shreds by the Demonata. Except Beranabus. He's strong enough to fight the demons as an equal, to survive among them. He's a few hundred years old. At least."

Raz and Sharmila have stopped arguing. Raz moves close to his master, in case he needs help. Sharmila comes to squat by Nadia and me, and listens as Nadia continues her explanations.

"The mages who wanted to fight the Demonata contacted Beranabus. He'd been fighting demons long before they came along, but usually in this universe. He saw it as his duty to prevent the stronger demons from building tunnels and crossing over. He focused on the demon masters — the ones who could destroy our world if they found a way across."

"Have you ever fought a demon master?" Sharmila asks Nadia.

"Not yet," she says and a troubled expression flits across her face. She falls silent and starts chewing her nails again, biting hard. Sharmila squeezes the younger woman's shoulder, then takes up the story. She has a soft but firm voice.

"The mages asked Beranabus to teach them his ways. They wanted to study his methods, so they could fight the stronger demons too. He told them he was not interested in being their teacher. But they were persistent. Dogged him. Begged to become his students, to learn, to help.

"Finally, because he was tired of being bothered, or because he thought they might serve some good, he agreed.

He let a few travel with him through this universe, showed them how to fight, helped them understand more about their enemies. They passed that knowledge on, teaching others how to destroy windows before they were fully formed, how to fight demons who made it through. Although often, when a demon crosses, it is better not to engage them directly, just try to limit the damage."

She pauses and shrugs stiffly. "That is not the way we like it, but it is the way it must be. There are too few of us to take risks. Better we avoid direct conflict, and prevent other crossings, than fight, perish and leave the demons free to come as they please. Some disagree with that and take the fight to the Demonata, but they do not last very long."

"*You* tried fighting when you were younger," Nadia says, and Sharmila nods. "That's why Beranabus recruited you. You and Raz have fought demons. He knows he can take advantage of your nobler nature." She chuckles drily and shoots Beranabus a dark look. I realise she doesn't like the ancient magician. Maybe even hates him. But in that case, why does she work for him? Before I can ask, Nadia picks up the story again.

"The mages called themselves the Disciples, to honour Beranabus. He didn't care about that, but to them it was important. It still is. Their followers have kept the name. There are never many Disciples — maybe forty or fifty at any time. They patrol the world, thwarting the plans of lesser demons, searching for other humans with powers like their own, to recruit, train and set against the Demonata."

"Mostly we act independently of the master," Raz says and all our heads bob up. He's standing over me, rubbing his hands together, smiling. "We were not properly introduced earlier. My name is Raz Warlo. This is Sharmila Mukherji. And Nadia Moore. We are — I'm sure I speak for us all — delighted to meet you, and will do all in our power to make you feel that you are among friends and allies."

Sharmila laughs shortly. "Always the diplomat, Raz."

"One of us needs to be," he laughs back, then squats. "As I said, the Disciples mostly act without orders from the master. He leaves us free to operate as we see fit. Occasionally, he'll assign one of us a task, perhaps to watch for signs of demonic activity in a certain area, or to come into this universe with him to fight. But mostly we follow our own path."

"Lucky you," Nadia says bitterly and shoots another harsh look at Beranabus.

"Are you his… slave?" I ask hesitantly.

"I might as well be," she spits, then smiles painfully. "No. Beranabus is a real son of a bitch, but I'm free to leave if I wish. I'm different from Raz, Sharmila and the rest of the Disciples — more gifted. Not necessarily more powerful, but I can…" She trails off and glances at Raz and Sharmila, who are staring at her curiously. They don't know this bit either.

Nadia sniffs. "It's not a secret. Beranabus didn't tell you because there wasn't time. He won't mind if I fill you in. And I think I should because it concerns you and Raz too. It's the reason you're here."

"I have been curious about that," Sharmila says, and though Raz says nothing, I can see that he's intrigued also.

Nadia rubs her arms, shivering slightly. "I've been with Beranabus a long time, maybe seven or eight years — though it's been a lot longer than that in the human world. When Beranabus recruited me, talking movies had just come into fashion. It was 1929."

We gawp at her. Sharmila covers her mouth with a hand. Raz blinks owlishly.

"*1929?*" I echo. "But you're so young."

"I've spent most of those seven or eight years here, where – as I've explained – time works differently."

"You mean you missed the Second World War?" Raz asks. "Rock and roll? The Beatles?"

"Beetles?" Nadia asks innocently.

"The Beatles. The biggest band in the world. They…" He stops, not sure how to explain the Beatles to somebody from 1929.

"Poor girl," Sharmila says, tears of pity in her eyes.

"It's not so bad." Nadia shrugs uncomfortably. "When we return to the human world, we stay in a cave which has been Beranabus's base for many centuries. I haven't seen the outside world since I joined him. I'm not jealous or regretful. Not really."

She tries to make it sound like she honestly feels that way, but it's clear that she's deeply unhappy.

"Why?" Raz asks softly. "Why did the master ask this great sacrifice of you? What is your gift?"

"Fortune-telling," Nadia says with a giggle. "I was a child fortune-teller. I'd dress up as a gypsy and read people's palms, tea leaves, a crystal ball — whatever. When my parents realised I could make money doing it, they set up a special room in our house. Later, they took me on the road with a travelling fair. I had a tent of my own. They billed me as Nadia Le Tarot. It was fun, but frightening sometimes — I could see people's death. I was supposed to just tell them good things, but if I saw something upsetting, I couldn't always hide it. That got me into trouble.

"I don't know how Beranabus found me. He just turned up one night, and whisked me off into the madness of this. I was terrified. I didn't know who he was or what he wanted. And all the demons…"

She shudders and glares at Beranabus. I try to imagine what that must have been like. It's not difficult, since I'm in much the same boat as she was. But at least I made the decision to come here.

"In time, I learnt why Beranabus took me," Nadia says. "I can sense things which have not yet happened. There are many people who claim that gift, but I'm one of the few who can really do it. Beranabus says my kind are even rarer than magicians."

"How much can you see?" Sharmila asks, and there's an edge to her voice. "Can you see when we will die? And by what means?"

Nadia shakes her head. "Not yet. I have to focus to gain insights like that. And I prefer not to. I don't like knowing such details."

"You say you can see the future before it happens," Raz says slowly. "But if that is true, surely you can act to change it."

"No. It's not that specific. I might, for instance, see that you'll die in a fire, but I won't know when or where it will happen. My insights are never something that can be altered. If I get a glimpse of a future event, it's because it has in some way already happened. It can't be undone or prevented.

"But it *is* possible to use my gift to our advantage — that is, to Beranabus's advantage." She goes quiet, staring at her fingernails. Most are bitten down to the quick, except the smallest nail on her left hand. Maybe she's saving it for an especially stressful moment.

"There is a weapon," Nadia whispers, and we have to lean in to hear. "A demonic weapon, maybe legendary, maybe real — Beranabus doesn't know. They call it the Kah-Gash. According to the legends it's ancient, even by the standards of the Demonata. We're talking millions of years. It was broken up into a number of pieces aeons ago and they've been missing ever since."

"How many pieces?" Raz asks.

"We don't know. We don't think any demon knows either. But certain demon masters have been looking for them ever since. Beranabus is searching for the pieces too. Because whatever the Kah-Gash is, the legends claim it has the power to destroy universes. They say it can wipe out either the universe of the Demonata and every demon in it — or our own, and everyone in that."

"What weapon could be so powerful?" Raz gasps. "Even a nuclear missile cannot destroy an entire universe."

Nadia shrugs. "If I had the answer, I'd know more than Beranabus or any of the Demonata. But I know this much — one of the pieces *will* soon be found. I've seen it." She starts chewing at the smallest nail on her left hand. "Beranabus has had me concentrating on the Kah-Gash ever since he brought me here. I spend hours of every day brooding about it, running the word through my thoughts, trying to find out where the pieces might be.

"A few days ago I had an insight. I sensed that part of the Kah-Gash was going to be discovered in the near future. I caught a glimpse of a demon — Cadaver. Words popped into my thoughts — 'The demon thief will guide you. Find the thief'."

Find the thief. That's what Mrs Egin said when she was freaking out, and just before she exploded! I start to tell the others, but Sharmila speaks up before me.

"Cadaver stole the baby — Kernel's brother."

Nadia nods. "Beranabus was ecstatic when that happened. It confirmed that we were on the right track, that Cadaver was a demon thief."

"So that's what this is about," Raz says, nudging my right arm. (It doesn't hurt now. It's been healed by magic.) "Nadia and the master came for me — having already collected Sharmila — a day or so ago. The master said he had need of me, but didn't say what he wanted me for. Now I see — it was to help search for the Kah-Gash."

"But I don't see what difference you or I can make," Sharmila frowns. "Were we in your vision, Nadia?"

"No."

"Then why involve us? If Beranabus has searched for this weapon by himself all these years, why come to us for help now?"

"Because of what I saw and sensed," Nadia mumbles. "If we pursue this, there will be a confrontation. I caught glimpses of a battle with forces greater than our own." She pulls her finger away from her mouth. Sets both hands on her knees. Looks at each of us slowly, one after the other, as she speaks. "Beranabus didn't tell you about this because there was no time. But I doubt he would have told you anyway, in case he frightened you away."

"I'm not frightened of a fight," Raz snorts.

"I am," Sharmila says. "But I would fight regardless, if Beranabus asked me. He knows that. I have fought before. Raz too. You said that is why he chose us."

"Yes. But it wasn't just a fight that I sensed." Nadia lowers her eyes and looks at the hands on her knees. They're trembling, but only slightly. She stares at them hard. When they stop trembling, she looks up at us and says directly, without any emotion, "I also sensed death."

OPENING WINDOWS

→Nadia falls silent. She squats with her face averted. Raz and Sharmila look anxious and move away to discuss the revelation in whispers. I stay where I am, watching Beranabus work. I'm not that disturbed by Nadia's prediction. This is all crazy anyway. Death's only to be expected in a place like this.

Beranabus is having difficulties with the window. The patches of light are slotting into place, but slowly. And while most of the patches he's joined together are pulsing at the same rate, some aren't. If he could see the lights, it would be simple, but he can't. He has to create the window using complicated, time-consuming spells.

I can't understand why the magician and the others can't see the lights. They're more powerful and experienced than me. So why am I the only one who can view the assembly of the window?

While I'm pondering that, a few more patches of light slot into place. A shimmer runs through the panel. The various colours vibrate a few times in unison. Then they all turn yellow and stop pulsing.

"Ah!" Beranabus grunts. He turns, claps his hands to get everyone's attention, then waves at the window of yellow light, now visible for all to see. Raz and Sharmila approach with suspicion. Nadia hangs back.

"Do you know what is through there?" Sharmila asks.

"Another world," Beranabus says.

"Can you be more specific?"

He shrugs. "I was searching for Cadaver, not a specific world. Until we pass through the window, I've no way of telling where we'll emerge." He raises a bushy eyebrow. "Nervous, Miss Mukherji?"

"Nadia told us about her vision," Raz mutters, gaze lowered. "About the Kah-Gash and your quest. She said there would be fighting and death."

Beranabus snorts. "That girl should learn to keep her mouth shut." He glares at Nadia, then shrugs. "You chance death every time you face a demon. That's nothing new."

"But we have been told that on this occasion it definitely lies in wait," Sharmila says. "That is different."

"Not really," Beranabus says. "Nadia has no idea who will die. It could be anyone — you, her, me, the boy. Maybe it will be all of us." Beranabus looks at the window and scowls. "You can quit if you wish. I've no time for cowards. But consider this — the Kah-Gash can destroy a universe. If you withdraw and the piece of the weapon we're chasing falls into the hands of the Demonata..."

"You really believe the Kah-Gash exists?" Sharmila asks.

"Aye."

Sharmila and Raz share an uneasy glance then Raz nods, followed — after a pause of several seconds — by Sharmila.

"How about you, Fleck?" Beranabus turns his small dark eyes on me. This is the first really close look I've had of him. His skin is pale, but covered in dirt and grime. Lots of wrinkles, and a few old scars and blemishes. Untidy black hair, clumps of grey and white, his beard trimmed unevenly. His hands are clean, in contrast with the rest of him, but the tight flesh round his knuckles is covered by lots of blotches and faded scars. Dusty, dirty clothes. He wears a small flower in a buttonhole on his jacket, which looks pathetically out of place. Several of his teeth are missing, and the rest are crooked and rotten. He smells bad, like something that has half decomposed. I don't like him and I don't trust him. But he's the only hope I have of finding Art.

"I'm coming," I say, trying to sound more positive than I feel.

"Then it's decided," Beranabus says and steps through the yellow window. Sharmila follows, then Nadia — reluctantly, chin low.

Raz claps me on the back. "After you."

I face the window of yellow light. Think about the demons that might be waiting on the other side. Take a breath. Hold it. Step through.

* * *

→A desert world. It's night, but lots of stars are glittering, so I can see clearly in all directions. Beranabus is magically searching for Cadaver, standing very still, eyes closed. After a few minutes he shakes his head. "He's been through here but didn't stop." Rolling his shoulders, he spits on his hands, scuffs the sand with his feet, then starts on another spell, to open a new window and follow the demon to whatever world it fled to next.

The patches of light round us are glowing steadily when Beranabus begins. Soon after he starts searching for Cadaver, several pulse and move towards a spot in front of him. As he chants, more pulse and others drift in from afar to be added to the patchwork panel. Beranabus is piecing them together with spells. But if he could see them like I could, and move them directly by hand...

I think about offering my help, but I'm afraid he'll laugh at me, so I keep my idea to myself. After a while I realise it's been ages since I ate or drank, yet I don't feel hungry or thirsty. I mention this to Raz, who's lying on the sand close by, idly gouging out shapes with a finger.

"I noticed that too," he says. "And although I have been here a day or two, I don't feel sleepy. Our bodies must work differently in this universe. It is a place of magic and you can do many incredible things with magic." He waves a hand over the sand and a sandcastle slowly thrusts upwards, turrets, a moat, tiny sandy guards on the ramparts.

"Cool!" I gasp. "Do you think I could...?"

"Try," he says. "I didn't know I could do that until just now."

Excited, I sit and think about a castle even bigger and grander than Raz's. I wave a hand over the sand, summoning my masterpiece.

Nothing happens.

Disappointed, I decide I'm being too ambitious, so I picture a smaller castle, with fewer turrets and troops. Again, nothing happens. I keep lowering my expectations, demanding less and less, until finally I ask for the simplest sandcastle possible. The sand ripples, then spits up a meagre glob.

Raz laughs. "Don't worry. Gifts vary. Magic shows itself uniquely in each person. I can create sandcastles. Perhaps you can change shape or make rain."

"Really?"

"It's possible."

I close my eyes and think about what sort of an animal I'd like to turn into.

→Later. No luck with the shape-changing or making rain. If I have a magical gift, it must be *very* unique!

Beranabus is hard at work on the window, which seems to be nearing completion. I'm lying next to Nadia, Sharmila and Raz close by. Nadia's been telling us about her life with Beranabus, the ways of demons, how to fight them.

"Where are they all?" I ask during a lull. "This is the second world I've been to, and apart from the trees, I haven't seen any demons."

"In a hurry to spot some?" Sharmila chuckles.

"No. I was just wondering. Where do they live?"

"They could be anywhere," Nadia says. "Beneath the sand. All around us and invisible. On the other side of the world. There might be thousands here or only one. It varies. Some demons create a world just for themselves. Others—"

"Demons can create worlds?" Raz interrupts.

"The stronger ones can. Most just rampage through existing realms, but demon masters have the power to make new worlds and even self-contained universes."

"Do they make the stars as well?" I ask.

Nadia smiles grimly. "Those aren't stars."

We stare at her then up at the sky. It's peppered with glowing dots. They're not like the stars in our universe — they're bigger, brighter, closer, and many move across the heavens like meteors. But they can't be anything other than...

"They're demons," Nadia says.

"They can't be!" Sharmila protests.

"Nevertheless, they are."

"But..." Sharmila gazes up at the sky, horrified. "To be able to see them from here ... they must be enormous!"

"Yes."

"Are they demon masters?" Raz asks.

"A few, perhaps, but most are just incredibly large demons who sail the skies, looking for others to torture and destroy. They don't usually bother with the likes of us – we're too tiny – but occasionally one might decide to squash us like ants." She chuckles humourlessly. "When that happens, you get out as quick as you can. There's nothing else you can do against a star-sized demon."

I gawp at Nadia, then at the sky, filled with monstrous shapes. Suddenly, this place feels a lot more dangerous than it did a few minutes ago.

→The next world is a giant, needle-shaped chunk of rock. The top is flat and lumpy, sixty or seventy feet in diameter. A hot wind howls round it, biting at us, threatening to rip us loose and cast us over the edge.

Beranabus curses and crouches. We copy him. "I've been here before," he says, speaking as quietly as he can, yet loud enough to be heard over the howling wind. "It wasn't somewhere I ever wanted to return to."

The anxiety in his tone affects us all, even Nadia, who starts murmuring the words of a spell — I think it's meant to protect us, or at least her.

"I'll keep the window to the other world open as long as possible," Beranabus says. "That way, if we come under attack, we can..." He stops. The yellow window of light has blinked out of existence. Beranabus growls and a look of disgust crosses his face.

"What's happening, master?" Raz asks nervously.

"We've been ensnared," Beranabus says, rolling up the sleeves of his jacket and shirt. "Cadaver's led us into a trap."

"Is he here?" Sharmila asks, looking round uneasily.

"No. He's not welcome in this place. But he must have tipped off the Kallin. They were waiting for us. They destroyed the window."

"Who are the Kallin?" Raz yells.

"Crawl to the edge," Beranabus says, turning away from us and sitting cross-legged. "Have a look. Nadia," he adds, "marshal them. Help them fight. Buy me time. I don't think I'll be able to open a new window fast enough, but let's not die cheaply."

He starts muttering spells, lips moving at a tremendous speed. Around him, patches of light pulse and blink, then move together, a bit faster than before, but not greatly so.

We look at each other then crawl towards the edge of the needle. The wind increases as we get closer. We lie flat on our stomachs, inching forward. I feel sick. I don't want to look over the edge. But I must.

I don't suffer from vertigo, which is good because it's a long drop. And I mean L-O-N-G! I can't see the base of the needle. It seems to be suspended in mid-air, and for all I know, it is. We're in a universe of demonic magic. Who says giant needles of rock need to be rooted to the ground?

But the stomach-churning drop isn't the worst thing. Slithering up the face of the rock are... *things*. Hundreds and thousands of small, long, black, hairy, spider-like creatures. Except they can't be spiders because they have no legs. They move more like worms. Slithering towards us, an army of them. The Kallin.

One of the monsters leans back and raises its face to us. I see dozens of tiny eyes and a wide mouth. As I watch, the mouth stretches like a snake's, the thing opening its jaws far wider than its body. There are fangs inside the mouth. More than I can count.

Something taps my shoulder. I scream, whipping round. But it's only Nadia. She grabs me before I roll off the top of the needle, drags me away from the edge to where Sharmila and Raz are waiting.

"We're in trouble," she says simply. "There are thousands, so we can't fight them. Our best hope is to block them. That means a barrier of energy, to keep them back."

"Will that work?" Raz asks.

"We'll soon find out. Now, we have a few minutes, so let's see what we have to work with. I want each of you to create a personal barrier. Imagine yourself at the centre of a bubble of energy. Let your magic flow into it. Once I have an idea of your power, I can coordinate a spell and unite our magic forces."

Sharmila and Raz close their eyes and focus. I don't have a clue what I'm doing, but I follow their lead. I concentrate, trying not to think about the Kallin, willing a barrier into place, praying I have more success than with the sandcastle.

A few seconds later Nadia says, "Let's see what we have."

I open my eyes and spot her throwing a punch at Raz. Her fist stops several inches short of his face. She tries again — same result. She grunts with satisfaction. Jabs at Sharmila. Her fist slows but doesn't stop. Lightly smacks into Sharmila's chin, not harming her but getting through the barrier. "Try to strengthen it," Nadia says. Jabs a second time. Again, she penetrates Sharmila's barrier, but with more difficulty. Pulls a so-so face.

"Now you," she says to me. Makes a fist, starts to throw a punch... then stops. Sticks out her right index finger. Pokes at me softly. Prods my nose. Smiles. "Guess you're out of this one."

"It's not my fault," I grumble. "I'm not used to magic. I don't know how to make it work."

"It's OK." She tweaks my nose. "You can be our second line of defence. Watch for any demons getting through. If one penetrates the barrier, do your best to kill it while we plug up the hole it creates."

"How do I kill them?" I ask.

"With magic. You can stamp on them, choke them, firebolts of energy — whatever comes most naturally to you. But there has to be magic as well. You can't kill a demon by physical force alone."

"What if I can't make it work? What if—"

"Kernel!" she snaps. "We don't have time for hysterics. Just do your best, like when you escaped from the demon tree."

She draws Sharmila and Raz aside to prepare them. While they're discussing magical barriers, I creep to the edge of the needle to monitor the advance of the Kallin. They're a lot closer than a couple of minutes ago. Not so small now that I have a better view of them. Two or three feet long. Making soft squeaking noises, barely audible over the roar of the wind.

I think about throwing myself off, taking the easy way out, not waiting for them to clamber over me and rip at me with their fangs. One short step or leap… a few seconds or minutes of freefall… then no more worries. Unless there's nothing to freefall to. Maybe there's no ground in this part of the Demonata's universe. I might bob back up or fall for ever, a lifetime of falling… screaming… thrashing.

"They're almost to the top!" I shout, putting the dark thoughts behind me. "Half a minute and they'll be all over us!"

"Get back here," Sharmila calls. They've gathered close to Beranabus, who's concentrating on the slowly forming window. I crouch next to Raz, feeling safer beside him than Sharmila, since he was able to construct a stronger barrier.

"Here we go," Nadia says shakily. She half closes her eyes. So do Sharmila and Raz. There's a shimmer in the air a couple of feet in front of us. Then nothing. I wonder if the spell has worked, if we're protected or not. Then the first of the Kallin wriggles over the edge of the needle and launches itself at us, mouth wide, fangs bared, screeching with hunger and hate.

FRYING PAN

→The demon flies straight at me, like an arrow fired from a bow. A scream builds at the back of my throat, but before it can burst out of my mouth, the Kallin hits an invisible barrier and is deflected. It crashes into a group of other long, hairy demons. Irritated, their fangs flash and they rip the first Kallin to shreds. Bloody bits of it fly everywhere.

I press myself hard against Raz as the demons surround us, gnashing at the barrier, wriggling around and over it, searching for weak points. Within seconds, they cover the barrier entirely, blocking our view of the sky, plunging us into almost total darkness. I can see by the light of the pulsing patches, but the others must be nearly blind.

Nadia clicks her fingers and a ball of flame appears overhead. I preferred the darkness. We can see the Kallin in more detail now, their long, hairy bodies, the stiff, spiky hairs on which they move, their abnormally large mouths and fangs. They drool and slobber as they snake across the face of the barrier. Soon it's like looking at them through a window streaked with spit and vile juices.

Raz is sweating. So are Sharmila and Nadia. Trembling, not with fear, but the effort of maintaining the barrier. This is hard. I don't think they can keep it up for more than a few minutes. I glance at Beranabus and the window he's working on. It's nowhere near complete. A few minutes won't be long enough.

One of the Kallin penetrates the barrier with its head. It squeals with triumph, fangs snapping together, trying to squeeze the rest of its body through. I tense, readying myself to fight, but then Nadia shouts a brief spell and the barrier closes sharply around the demon, slicing its head off.

The head falls to the floor, but the jaws continue snapping open and shut. It drags itself forward using its fangs, dozens of eyes glittering angrily. I get to my knees, face the head, try summoning magic to use against it. Instead, panic-stricken, I throw up. The demon gibbers — it can still make noise — and crawls at me through the pool of vomit. I watch, repulsed and terrified. Then, as it's about to drag itself out of the vomitous pool, I have a thought. I reach out, touch the vomit with a finger and charge it with magic, which flows through me from some unknown source.

The vomit bubbles and becomes acid. The Kallin head shakes wildly. Desperate, it hurls itself out of the pool, using an upper fang as a makeshift vaulting pole. I make a fist and, roaring with fear, punch the head back down. The acid eats into it. The head shakes a few more times, then dissolves, bubbling away to a bloody, hair-streaked mess.

A feeling of power and victory washes through me. I've killed a demon! I used magic to destroy its ugly ass! I'm Hercules, Samson and Thor rolled into one! I glare at the thousands of Kallin, eager for another to break through, so I can send it the way of its boiled-down brother. "Come on," I snarl. "I'll turn you all into stew!"

"The boy's enjoying himself," Raz notes, teeth chattering from the effort of keeping the barrier in place.

"I do not think he will be so... anxious to fight... when the barrier breaks... and they come crashing down upon us... in their multitudes," Sharmila mumbles.

Nadia says nothing. She's staring ahead, eyes wide open now, sweat filling the pockmarks on her face. Terrified.

Overcome with confidence, forgetting that moments ago I was throwing up and more afraid than I'd ever been, I take matters into my own hands. Turning to where Beranabus is piecing together a window, I watch the pulsing lights for a couple of seconds. Then, impatient, I reach up and nudge a patch of light towards the cluster. It slides ahead of my fingers, slotting into place. I start moving others. It's simple. I don't even have to touch the lights — they move before my fingers, weightless, a breeze to manipulate.

"What are you doing?" Beranabus snaps.

"I can do it quicker than you," I tell him, adding more patches of light to the now rapidly forming window.

"You're distracting me," Beranabus growls. "Get out of my way before—"

"You're too slow!" I shout. "You can't see the lights. I can. So let me do it. I can make…" I pause. The lights around me have stopped pulsing. For a second — absolute panic. I can't complete the window! Then I realise what's happened. "Where were you trying to open the window to?" I pant. Beranabus starts to argue. "Just tell me!" I yell.

Beranabus squints then says, "I was searching for Cadaver."

I think about the demon which stole my brother. Recall its long legs, stumpy body, thick hairy fingers. Its face, half human, half canine. Its drooping ears and wide white eyes.

The patches of light start pulsing again. Eagerly, I reach up and begin slotting them into place, creating a window. I'm not sure how or why this works, but I *know* I'm right. I was never crazy. The lights weren't imaginary. They were there for a reason — and now that reason is clear. I can't use magic to make sandcastles or barriers, but I can sure as hell open windows to other worlds!

Beranabus stares at me wordlessly. He can't see the lights. He only sees my hands moving swiftly, fingers flying in all directions, like a mad conductor. But he feels the magic. He knows – hopes – I'm not blowing our only chance of survival.

"Master!" Raz shouts.

"Hush," Beranabus says. "Let him work. If he can do what I think…"

"But the barrier!" Raz cries. "We cannot hold it! I feel it crumbling!"

Beranabus mutters a quick spell and I sense the barrier thicken around us. The cries of the demons and howl of the wind are muted slightly.

"Relax," Beranabus says to me. "I can hold this barrier for a long while now that I have nothing else to focus on. You have time."

I don't respond or slow down. Too excited. I can see the window coming together. For the first time in my life I feel completely in control of myself and the world around me. I have a purpose. I know what I was born for. This is my gift. Why I always felt like a misfit. I had a great power. A destiny.

"What's he doing?" Nadia asks.

"Something I've never seen anyone else do," Beranabus says softly. "Not even the most powerful demon master."

"Are you sure he is not having some kind of fit?" Sharmila asks.

"We're dead if he is," Beranabus laughs.

"I don't like this, master," Raz says. "To place our lives in the hands of an untested child…"

"Children are often the true saviours," Beranabus says. "Not knowing the rules of the universes, they can sometimes turn those rules on their head. We must trust, Raz Warlo. And hope." I feel his eyes hot on my back. "The boy is all we have."

I don't think about my grave responsibility. All I focus on are the patches of light, pulsing in the air around me, more gliding into reach from the world outside, slipping through the ranks of Kallin and the wall of the barrier. Nothing can hold the lights back, interfere with them or divert them from their course. Except me. I'm their master. I can do anything with them that I like.

My hands blur. The panel of lights builds, two feet wide, three feet high... four... five. Just as I'm adding a large, hexagonal block of blue light to the mass, the lights pulse in unison a few times, then go a dull shade of steady white.

"By all the gods!" Raz gasps.

"I do not believe it!" Sharmila exclaims.

"No!" Nadia moans with disbelief.

Beranabus just chuckles and says, "My compliments, Kennel."

"It's Kernel," I correct him, looking up at his bearded face and small dark eyes. "Kernel Fleck. Master of the lights."

He tilts his head, acknowledging my power. I've never felt more alive or special. The others gawp from me to the window, then back at me.

"How?" Nadia asks.

Beranabus speaks before I can. "Let's save the explanations for when we're not surrounded by thousands of demons." He stares at the writhing ranks of the Kallin. Smiles. Then steps through the window of light. I glance at the others, grinning proudly. They're smiling too now.

One last look at the Kallin. They're screeching louder than ever, furious at us for escaping their trap. Laughing, I flip them the finger, then face the window of light and eagerly step forward after Beranabus, figuring nowhere in the universe can be as bad as this place.

Wrong!

FIRE

→I know instantly that we're in trouble. Beranabus is fighting a variety of demons, snake-like, but with arms and claws, heads of tigers, lions, vultures. Several are locked in battle with the elderly magician, ripping at him with talons and fangs, moving incredibly fast. He's striking back with bolts of lightning. A couple of demons are lying in pieces around him. But there are more to come.

In the distance, I spot another window and a demon leaving through it. I'm not certain, but I think it's Cadaver! In a rush of excitement I start towards the window, but then one of the other demons spots me. Shrieks like a bird of prey. Lashes backwards with its scaly tail, driving itself at me. I freeze, losing my new-found confidence. Looking past the demon, I see the window come apart and I lose hope too. Cut off from my prey, isolated and terrified, I stand motionless and defenceless.

Raz steps through the window behind me. Yells with surprise and fear, then pushes ahead of me and grabs the attacking demon by its arms. Sinks his teeth into its throat.

Bites it open, then spits the slimy flesh out. Puts his teeth up close to the hole in the thrashing demon's throat. Blows into it — but magic comes out of his mouth, not air. Enters through the gash. The demon explodes. Raz tosses its remains aside and moves to deal with the next in line.

Sharmila steps through, then Nadia. Sharmila gasps, looks around in wild terror, then gains control and steps up beside Raz. A jackal-headed demon leaps on her. She thrusts a hand at its stomach. As soon as she touches it, flames burst from her fingers. Seconds later, the demon's on fire, writhing in the dust.

Nadia curses, starts forward, then looks back at me. "Shut the window!"

"But… we have to go back… we can't stay here… there are—"

"The barrier won't hold now that we've moved on!" she shouts. "If you don't close it, the Kallin will be able to follow us through!"

I hate turning my back on the fighting, but I can't ignore her warning. I stare at the window of white light, not sure what to do. So I try the first thing that comes into my head. Reach into the window, to rip it apart. But my hands slide through the light and nothing happens.

I can't see anything through the window, but I imagine the Kallin massing on the other side. They could come slithering through at any second. I should run, get away from here, flee for my…

I force myself to take a breath. Consider the problem. It was easy to put the patches of light together, so it must be easy to take them apart. But how?

I begin to reach into the window again. Pause. Half close my eyes and study it carefully. Although it looks like a solid wall of light, if I squint, I can make out thin lines where the original patches join. Tiny cracks running through the window, almost invisible. I run my index finger round one of the larger patches near the centre, thinking. Then, without trying to touch it, I slide my finger at the patch from the side, willing it to move.

The patch comes loose and glides away from my finger, becoming a pulsing strawberry colour. After a few seconds it stops pulsing, hangs in the air a moment, then drifts away.

I work on freeing other patches. After removing about a dozen, the window disintegrates. The patches regain their original colours and slide away from one another in a slow, graceful explosion.

No time for pride. I check what's happening with the demons. There aren't as many as on the needle of rock, but they're larger and stronger, and there's no time to construct a barrier to keep them at bay.

They're all around Beranabus and his Disciples. A few have caught hold of Raz and dragged him to the ground. He's lashing out with his fists, trying to chew their throats open. But they worry him like savage hounds. One rips off most of his right leg and devours the flesh, howling with satisfaction.

A claw strikes his head and slices half his face away. He tries to scream, but he no longer has a tongue.

I cry out with pity and terror, but there's nothing I can do to help the fat black man who was so nice to me, who saved my life mere moments ago. He's stronger than me. He knows how to fight demons. A true being of magic. If he can't handle these monsters, what hope do I have?

My eyes dart from Raz to the others. More than a dozen demons are at war with Beranabus. Five are focused on Sharmila. Nadia is fending off several more, making the ground explode in front of them, hitting them with bolts of magic, roaring hatefully like I do when I fight.

Two more barrel towards me, tails whipping from side to side, snarling, arms and claws extended.

Driven by desperate instinct, I reach towards two patches of purple and orange light. I clap my hands together, driving the patches hard at each other. They smash together and create a blinding flash of purplish-orangey light. The instinct which told me to try this also tells me to close my eyes — sharpish!

When I look a few seconds later, the demons are down, screaming with pain and confusion, eyes melted in their sockets.

I'm stunned by the power I've unleashed. Confidence comes flooding back. Once again I'm Kernel Fleck — defeater of the Demonata!

Then one of the fallen demons scrapes the gooey mess clear of its empty sockets. New globes grow, the demon using magic to construct a fresh pair of eyes. I realise I've only slowed the creatures down, not put them out of action for ever. Different universe — different rules.

Panic sets in again. The Disciples are doomed. Beranabus is finished. Cadaver set another trap for us and there's no way out of this one. My choice is simple — perish with the others or save myself.

I don't think of anywhere specific. I merely scream with all my inner senses — "*Somewhere safe!*" When nothing happens, I add rapidly, "Earth! A city!" Patches of light pulse around me. Frantic, I push them together, forming a new window as quickly as I can. I don't look up or think about the demons which might be bearing down on me. Focus on the lights.

I'm working quicker than I did on the needle, learning all the time, feeling power bubble through me. Then, out of the corner of my eye, I catch a glimpse of a demon lurching at me. I flinch but don't stop. The demon rushes closer... closer... It's one of the pair I blinded. Seething for revenge. A few more seconds and it'll be on me. I should turn to deal with it, but my hands won't stop moving. There's nothing I can do.

Then the demon's knocked aside. It grunts heavily, then screams. I can't see what's happening to it and I don't look. Keep working on the window. Sweating heavily. Mouth dry. Weeping softly.

Something steps up beside me. I cry out, expecting the worst. But it's not a demon. It's Nadia. "Hurry!" she hisses. "Get us out of here!"

"I'm trying," I groan, hands a whir of motion.

Nadia stands with her back against mine, protecting me. I work faster, desperate to be out of here, somewhere real and normal, where demons can't get me.

The lights pulse together a few times, then turn red. A window opens.

"Nadia!" I shout.

"Good work." She yells Beranabus's name, then Sharmila's.

I look around. I can't see Beranabus — he's completely surrounded by demons. Sharmila's losing her battle too — six of the monsters are on her and although a few are aflame, she can't fight them off. She's lost an arm at the elbow. Bleeding from deep wounds. Panting heavily, with the wild look of a horse caught in a thunderstorm.

Raz is dead. A pair of demons have torn his head off. As I watch, they rip it in two then each retreats with half, dipping their foul jowls into his skull, scooping out his brains with their fangs and tongues. I get sick again, though there isn't much to come up this time.

"Let's go," Nadia says, taking my right arm.

"What about the others?" I cry.

"We can't help them."

"But..." I stare at her. Although my plan was to flee by myself, now that she's voiced it, I don't want to. I don't care much about the aloof Beranabus, but Sharmila has been a true friend. She tried to stop Cadaver stealing Art. We should help her, free her, take her with us.

"I'm going," Nadia snarls. "You do what you like." And, releasing my hand, she ducks through the window, disappearing in an instant.

I hesitate, torn between escape and nobility. Then a demon catches sight of me and slithers across. It has a vulture's head. There are bits of Raz's brains dripping from its beak.

Something within me snaps. Cowardice triumphs. And without any shame, I turn my back on the demons – and Beranabus and Sharmila – and dive through the window after Nadia.

ADRIFT

→A busy city street. Nadia's lying on the pavement. A woman and child are getting to their feet close by. She must have knocked them over when she crossed into this world. Other people are staring at us and the window of red light, mouths open. Cars are slowing as they pass, drivers and passengers captivated by the spectacle.

"Close it!" Nadia yells. I don't need telling twice. Before the vulture-headed demon can follow us, I dismantle the window.

Nadia's on her feet. As soon as the red light vanishes, she grabs me and runs. We race through the crowd of startled bystanders. Nobody tries to stop us.

We turn a corner, race down another busy street. Nadia leads me across the road, weaving through traffic, wincing at the blaring horns but otherwise taking no notice of the cars. Another corner, then another. Finally, in a quiet alley, she stops, releases me, squats beside a wall, leans her head against it, stares up at the clear blue sky — and whoops.

"We did it! You're a genius, Kernel! You got us out!" She looks at me with happy tears in her eyes. "I don't know how I'll ever repay you."

I smile at Nadia, then frown and look around nervously.

"It's all right," Nadia reassures me. "They can't track us. We're safe. We're alive!"

"Raz isn't," I note quietly.

Nadia's smile dims. "That was a shame. I liked Raz."

"And what about Beranabus and Sharmila?" I ask, guilt setting in. "We ran out. Left them to the demons. We should go back and—"

"No!" Nadia snaps. "No going back." Her eyes glitter. I take a step backwards — she looks like she's going to attack. She notices my fear and relaxes. "Don't worry. I won't hurt you. But we're not going back. We couldn't do any good if we did."

"But... the others?"

She shrugs. "Beranabus will probably survive. He's come through worse. He'll wriggle free somehow. As for Sharmila..." She sighs. "Maybe Beranabus will save her. Maybe not."

She stands and looks at the sky. Lightly runs a finger across her cheeks, caressing the spots and acne scars. "It's warm. Must be late spring or summer. Maybe it's June. That's my favourite month. It's when I was born and when Beranabus took me. I was out walking, a perfect June day, dreaming about my birthday, presents and the future.

Looking forward to growing up. I was a plain child, dowdy. But my father said I was an ugly duckling, that I'd turn into a beautiful, glamorous swan one day.

"I was thinking about that – longing for it – when Beranabus spirited me away. Dropped me into the universe of the Demonata. Explained how important I was, all the lives I could save, the good I could do. Offered me no choice. Robbed me of my dreams of a happy future."

Nadia's expression darkens. "He shouldn't have taken me so young. I hadn't seen enough of the world. If he'd come when I was older, I'd have joined him gladly. But taking me like he did... stealing me like that demon stole your brother... it was wrong. Don't you agree, Kernel?"

I stare at her uncertainly. Now that she's mentioned Art, it drives home the fact that I didn't just run out on Beranabus and Sharmila. I deserted my brother too. Left him in that nightmarish universe. Alone in the hands of Cadaver.

"We have to go back," I say softly.

Nadia doesn't hear — or pretends she doesn't. "I wonder where we are?" she says brightly. "London? New York? Paris? Vienna? The world's changed so much since I left, I suppose I wouldn't recognise the cities I visited when I was younger. But there must be parts which are the same. I hope this is–"

"Nadia," I interrupt. "We have to go back. Find them. Help them if they're still fighting, link up with them if they've escaped."

"And if they're dead?" she answers, not looking at me.

"I don't know. Search for Art by ourselves, I guess."

She laughs. "You're brave but stupid, Kernel. You wouldn't last five minutes in that universe without Beranabus. You're good at opening windows but not at fighting. What would you do if you caught up with Cadaver? He'd rip you to shreds without breaking a sweat."

"But... Art... I have to—"

"Your brother's dead," Nadia growls. "Cadaver probably killed him on that first world and fed his body to one of the trees."

"No," I moan. "He's alive. I sense it."

"You *want* to sense it," she corrects me. "You want him to be alive, so you've convinced yourself he is. But think about it. Why wouldn't Cadaver kill him? He was on the run. He wouldn't have time to play nursemaid to a squalling baby."

A kid on a skateboard turns into the alley and whizzes past us. Nadia stares at the skateboard, head cocked, probably in much the same way that I stared when I first saw a demon.

"I've missed so much," she mutters. "The world's moved on while I've been fighting. So many places to see. So many things to do. Is it true you can fly anywhere now, in aeroplanes?"

"Nadia," I try again, "Beranabus needs us. We can't abandon him."

"Why not?" she retorts. "You've only known him five minutes. He treated you like a slave, the way he treats everyone. What do you owe him? Why throw your life away on his account?"

"I need him to help get Art back. I can't—"

"Stop talking about your brother like he's alive!" Nadia shouts. "Let him go. Admit he's dead. Move on. You can go home — I'll help find your parents. Forget about the Demonata. Pretend it was a bad dream. That's what I'm going to do."

"I can't," I say stubbornly. "Art's alive and I'm going to find him."

"You'll go back?" she asks mockingly. "Face the demons? Die like Raz? You didn't know what you were stepping into when you followed us through the first window. Now you're better informed. Do you really have the courage to cross universes freely?"

"I have to," I mutter. "For Art."

"I don't think so," Nadia says coldly. "You ran. The time to fight has passed. You feel guilty because you didn't stand by Beranabus and you want to put things right. But if you think it through, you'll see that's madness. You don't want to go back. And you won't. You'll stay in this universe, where you're safe. Like me."

I stare at the ground, tears creeping down my cheeks. Everything she says is true. I am afraid. I don't want to go back. I'm a coward.

But despite all my weaknesses, I have to return. Because I love Art more than I fear demons.

"Come with me," Nadia says, taking my hands. She's smiling, looking prettier than normal, hair shining in the sun. "I'll take you back to your parents if you want or you can stay with me. I'll be a sister to you. We can travel the world together. I'll use my gift to make money. We'll stay in the best hotels, sail the seas on mighty liners, fly through the sky on aeroplanes. Anything you want, I'll give you. It will be a precious life. No worries, no fears, no demons."

I shake my head slowly. "I can't," I croak. "Art's my brother. I can't abandon him."

Nadia scowls and releases my hands. "Have it your own way, fool! But when you're dying beneath some hideous demon, watching it reel your guts out like a cat playing with a ball of string, remember what I offered you."

She turns on her heel and marches away.

"Nadia!" I cry. "Where are you going?"

"There," she says, waving a hand at the world in general.

"Don't leave me," I wail. "I don't know where we are. You have to help me find Beranabus. You can go after that, but…"

She turns a corner and storms out of sight, leaving me in the alley. Alone.

→I'm sitting on the dusty ground. Hands on my knees. Head on my hands. Crying. It's been maybe an hour since Nadia left. I kept thinking she'd come back, that she'd decide she couldn't desert me. But there's been no sign of her. And the more I think about what she said, and her face when she said it, the less chance I think there is of her returning. Nadia hated her life with Beranabus. She went along with him because she had no other choice. But then I gave her a way out and she leapt at it.

Eventually, when the tears stop, I get to my feet and look around. I feel hungry now that I'm back in my own world, but there's no time to eat. I have to find Beranabus — if he's still alive.

There are dozens of patches of light hanging in the air around me, but none are pulsing. I wipe my cheeks clean, then focus. "Beranabus," I mutter, thinking about his face, his shabby suit, the flower in the buttonhole, his clean hands. I repeat his name, over and over, waiting for the lights to pulse.

Nothing happens. The lights maintain their steady glow.

I go cold — maybe that means he's dead!

"Art," I say quickly, fixing my brother's features in my mind. I concentrate on his name and face, but the lights don't change.

My stomach's tight with fear. Are they both dead, slaughtered by demons? They must be. Otherwise, why wouldn't the lights pulse and lead me to them?

I have another thought, just before panic sets in completely. I visualise Cadaver's horrible features and say the demon's name, time and time again. Nothing.

The fear drains out of me as I realise the lights work differently here. They don't pulse when I think of a person or place. The magician and my brother might still be alive.

Relief floods through me — then drains almost immediately. Because if the lights don't work the same way here, how will I find Beranabus or Art, or open a window to the universe of the Demonata?

I can't get back.

PUNKS

→Wandering the streets of the city. It's been a long time since I was in a place this crowded and noisy. I missed city life when I was living in Paskinston. I remembered only the good things — cinema, swimming pools, parks, school. I forgot about the traffic, the towering buildings that cut out the sunlight, the isolation.

I was always with Mum or Dad when I lived in the city, or with a teacher or babysitter. But one day, on a school trip to a museum, I got lost. It was an hour before I was found. I remember now what that felt like, how scary it was, how I believed I'd be lost for ever. I was sure I'd have to sleep on a park bench or underneath a bridge like a homeless person. It was terrifying.

This is scarier. At least then I knew what city I was in, but this could be anywhere. None of the street names or buildings is familiar. I think about asking an adult where I am, but I don't want to appear out of place. If I go up to a stranger and they learn that I'm lost, that I don't even know what city I'm in, they'll take me to the police. And while part of me would love that – the police would arrange for me to be sent home – I can't go down that route. If the police take me into custody, I won't be free to search for Art.

I haven't given up on my brother. The lights might not work the same way as in that other universe, but I can still see them. There must be a way for me to start the patches pulsing. I just have to figure it out.

While I'm puzzling over the problem, I continue walking. I listen carefully to people talking. Most speak the same language as me, but the accents aren't familiar. I wish again that I could ask where I am, but it isn't possible.

I'm growing hungrier with every step. I've drunk plenty of water from drinking fountains, but I've had nothing to eat. I pass a stall selling hot dogs and pretzels. I root through my pockets, but I don't have any money. I think about trying to steal a pretzel, but if the owner catches me it could mean *big* trouble.

Stomach growling, tears tickling the corners of my eyes, I walk on.

→My watch is working again. I've been here at least two hours, wandering without direction. The sun is starting to set. It will be night soon. Where will I sleep?

Time to sit and think this through. I find a bench in a small park. I'm shivering. Though it's not especially cold, I'm only wearing a T-shirt, no jumper. There aren't many people in the park. One woman who passes looks at me closely. I think she's going to stop and ask if I'm OK. I'm not sure what to say if she does. I was never a good liar. But then she carries on, deciding I'm not her business.

I try to lay all my problems out nice and simply, so I can think them through one at a time. My main priority is getting back to the Demonata's universe. But that will have to wait. Things I have to settle first — Where am I? Where will I sleep tonight? How will I find food?

Take them one at a time. Location. I can't find out by asking passers-by but there must be alternatives. A library, perhaps, except I don't know where to find one. But now that I set my mind to it calmly, I see there are other ways. I can look in a telephone book in a phone box. Or go into a newsagent's and read the titles of the local papers.

I manage a small chuckle when I realise how simple it is to place myself. That gives me confidence and I turn to the other problems more positively. I can dig through rubbish bins for food. Not very nice, but I'm sure I'll scavenge enough to keep myself from starving.

Finding somewhere to sleep is harder. Hide in a library or museum? Or maybe in a shop that sells furniture? Keep low while they're closing, then come out when it's deserted, sleep on a couch or bed.

Not a bad plan, except all the shops have already closed. I might be able to do it tomorrow, but it won't work now. Maybe I'll have to sleep in the open tonight, over a street grille or on a park bench. Collect newspapers to wrap round myself. Hope I'm not discovered by a policeman. Look for somewhere better in the morning.

As I'm thinking that over, I catch sight of a pulsing light out of the corner of my left eye. My head jerks towards it. This isn't the first time it's happened. I've been reacting to every flashing light in shops or on street corners, hopes rising, thinking for a second that they're one of the magical pulsing patches.

I scowl at myself, feeling stupid for falling for the same trick for the hundredth time. I start to look away, telling myself to behave more sensibly next time, when it strikes me —

There's no shop or street corner where the flash came from.

I look left again, but slowly, not letting myself get excited. It's probably somebody on a bicycle, or a bird with a strip of foil in its beak, or…

But it isn't. It's a yellow patch of triangular light, drifting through the park, attached to nothing.

I'm on my feet immediately, thoughts of food and shelter forgotten, hurrying after the light. I catch up to it, reach for it like a baby reaching for its dummy, then stop. There's no point interfering with it, since there are no other pulsing patches for me to add it to. Better to follow, see where it leads and hope that luck is with me.

* * *

→The light passes through the bars at the rear of the park. I clamber over them, almost spearing myself on the spikes at the top, ripping the back of my T-shirt. I start to follow it across the road behind the park, but the driver of an approaching car blows his horn, warning me back. I wait impatiently for him to pass, then hurry after the light. Luckily, it's not moving very fast, so I soon catch up.

I walk along beside the patch until it passes through the wall of a building. I stare at the wall for a moment, lost, then look backwards, judging the path of the light. It's come at an angled line from the park. If it continues in that direction, it should come out again at some point to my right on the other side of the building.

I race round the building to the back. Advance to the point where I think the light will emerge, then stand, clenching my hands into fists, waiting, counting the seconds off inside my head. Five… eight… ten… fifteen… twenty-one…

The light reappears on the count of twenty-three, further to my right than I'd calculated. Grinning, I jog over, catch up with it, walk with it to the wall of another building, then quickly make my way to the rear, to wait for it again.

→I eventually lose the light at a collection of warehouses. There's no way for me to get to the rear before the light re-emerges. But that's not a worry. Because I've spotted other lights, floating through the air from different directions, all angling towards the same spot several hundred yards ahead of me. I can't see where they meet because of the buildings, but I have a good sense of where it is, so I weave through the streets. There's no need to bother with the lights any more, just head for the point of intersection.

Ten minutes later I round a corner and see a handful of lights penetrating the walls and roof of a large building in the middle of a row of restaurants, pubs and shops. There are people in front of the building, waiting to get in. As I edge closer I see that they're mostly teenagers dressed in leather jackets, ripped jeans, fishnet stockings. Many have spiky, coloured hair and chains dangling from their ears, noses and lips. They look quite frightening. Not as frightening as demons, but pretty scary as humans go.

I hear music coming from inside the building and realise this is a concert. It's harsh, ugly music, loud and unpleasant, very fast. It sets my ears ringing, even from this far outside.

I stop close to the crowd. There are a couple of men at the front door, dressed differently. They're the ones in charge, taking money from the people who want to go to the concert, letting in a few at a time. As I watch, the doormen turn away a girl and three boys. A row develops. I hear the girl shouting that they're over eighteen. One of the doormen laughs and tells them to produce ID or leave.

This isn't going to be easy. If they won't let those four in, they certainly won't let in someone like me. I'll have to try a bluff, say that my dad — maybe an older brother would be better — is in there. It probably won't work, but I've got to give it a go.

I listen to the teenagers chatting about the concert, gathering as much info as I can. They call it a punk concert. There are several bands on the bill. Names like the Clamps, Thunderballs, the Damnable. When I'm ready, I walk boldly to the front of the line and smile at the doormen. "Excuse me," I say politely. "Is this where the Clamps are playing?"

The doormen squint at me. One grunts, "Yeah. But it's over-eighteens."

"I know," I reply. "But my brother's in there. I need to find him. Mum and Dad have gone out for the night. He was supposed to leave the key to the back door for me, but he must have taken it with him. I can't get in without it. Can I pop in and get the key off him? I'd leave again immediately."

The doormen look at each other, then one of them says, "What's his name?"

I'm about to say Art, but that's not a common name. So I say "John" instead.

"John what?" the doorman asks.

Again, Fleck isn't common, so I say the first name that comes to me. "Smith."

"John Smith." The doormen laugh.

"You've got to admire his nerve," one of them says.

"Yeah, but not enough to let him in," the other chuckles, then jerks his thumb at me. "Nice try. Now clear off."

"You don't understand," I gasp. "I can't get in without the key. I have to—"

"I can look for him if he really exists," the first doorman cuts in. "But if I go in there and call for a John Smith and don't find one – or find a few who aren't your brother – I'm going to be *very* angry. So have a good long think about it, then tell me — do I stay or do I go?"

"You don't have to do that. I'll look for him. He's a bit... he's slightly deaf. He wouldn't hear you calling. I need to go in myself, to look for..."

The doorman takes a step forward, crouches and in a low, foul curse tells me to go away. Then he returns to his post and waves forward the next few punks in line.

I've blown it. Defeated, I slink away, ignoring the catcalls of the punks, and find a quiet spot where I can think up my next approach.

→More lights are floating into the building, faster now. I could wait until the concert's over, then break in, but I don't think I have much time. So I go looking for another entrance, figuring there must be a fire door at the rear.

A narrow, dirty alley runs behind the shops and pubs. Rubbish bags all over the place, empty cardboard boxes, bottles and cans. Dried blood, vomit and dog crap. I wade through the mess, trying to find the building where the concert's taking place. The noise guides me and a minute later, I'm standing outside a pair of large doors, which are rattling from the vibrations of the music.

I try opening the doors, but they're locked from the other side. I push and pull, kick and punch, to no effect. I look for windows to sneak through, but there are only a couple and they're both bricked over.

Back to the doors. They can't remain shut all night. People will have to come through eventually. I'm sure they'll be opened at the end of the concert, but that might be too late — the lights may have stopped by then. I just have to hope that someone comes through before that, for fresh air or to be sick.

There are a few rubbish bins to the right of the doors. I crouch behind them and wait, planning on sneaking in if the doors open. Not a great plan, but in the absence of anything better, it's my only hope.

→Ten minutes pass. Fifteen. Twenty. Thirty. I'm truly cold now. I don't think the sun has ever shone directly on this horrible hole of an alley. My nose is running. I wipe the back of my hand across it, but that doesn't do much good.

The lights are moving very quickly, in greater numbers, powering through the walls and roof. I think a window is going to open soon. Maybe there's a witch like Mrs Egin inside, or perhaps the music is summoning the demons — this is the sort of din I imagine the Demonata would love.

Maybe some of them are coming to check out the concert.

I grin as I picture Cadaver and the vulture-headed demon slipping through a window between the two universes to dance with the punks. As I'm grinning, the doors open and two men step out into the alley, a wave of metallic music bursting through with them. I'm immediately alert, praying for them to turn left so I can duck in without them seeing.

But they stand where they are, looking around. One is a punk, with jeans, a leather jacket, no T-shirt, a thin black scarf knotted around his throat, spiky purple hair, a ring through his nose. Scrawny. Not much older than me. The other is wearing an army-type uniform, boots and a beret. A bit older than the punk and much bigger. There are letters tattooed on his knuckles, but I can't read them from here.

"This will be our getaway route if we have to run," the man in the army clothes says, letting the doors half close, cutting out the worst of the noise. "We'll split up if we're chased. You go left. I'll take the right. Meet again at the hotel."

"Can we outrun it?" the punk asks.

"Depends on what it is. Some are slow, some fast. If we can't stop it crossing, we'll try to fight, but if it's too strong, we'll have to run like hell."

"I don't like running," the punk says.

"Me neither," the army guy grunts, "but sometimes it's the only option. These demons are fierce mothers. We can whup some of them, but others…"

At the mention of demons, a shudder of relief churns through me. In a rush, I scuttle out from behind the rubbish bins. The army guy takes a step back, fists coming up protectively. The punk puts out a hand to calm him. "Relax. It's only a kid."

The army guy scowls. "What are you doing here? Trying to sneak in to the concert without paying? It won't work. Scram, you no-good—"

"Excuse me," I interrupt, "but are you… this might sound crazy… but I heard you talking about demons and I—"

"You heard nothing!" the army guy shouts. "Now beat it, quick, before I—"

"Wait a minute," the punk says, squinting at me with pale blue eyes. He nods for me to continue.

"Well… like I said… I heard you talking and… well… are you two guys… by any chance… I mean… are you Disciples?"

The pair stare at me dumbly. Then the army guy looks round, picks up a piece of metal, lets the doors swing almost fully closed, sticks the metal between them to keep them ajar. Strides over, the punk a couple of paces behind him.

"Who are you?" he growls.

"My name's Kernel Fleck. I was with Beranabus. I want to get back to him. I… Do you know who I mean? Are you…?"

The pair exchange silent glances. I start to think I got it wrong, that I misheard, or maybe the Demons are just

another band. But then the army guy shrugs and the punk
sticks out a hand. "Yes," the punk says as we shake hands.
"We're Disciples. This is Shark. And my name's Dervish.
Dervish Grady. But don't ask me to whirl," he says warningly.
And smiles.

THE MONSTER MASH

→Dervish starts to question me, to find out why I'm here, how I know Beranabus. But Shark cuts in. "The attack could come at any minute. We need to prepare for it."

He pulls the doors open and gestures me inside. It's dark and incredibly noisy. The room's quite large, but packed with punks. Mostly guys, Dervish's age or a bit older. A band is playing on a small stage to our right. Thrashing away at their guitars and drum kit as though the world is about to end and they're determined to finish their song before it does. The singer screams into his microphone, mostly swear words, sticking his middle fingers up at the crowd and bellowing at them.

The punks love it. They're dancing like crazy, leaping up and down or holding on to each other and spinning wildly. Some are fighting, but it's good natured. They're drawing blood, but they don't care — that just adds colour.

There are more studs, piercings and tattoos than I've ever seen. That reminds me of Shark's knuckles and I look down at his hands. His name is tattooed on both sets, a letter per finger, with a black and white shark's head filling the flesh between both thumbs and index fingers, jaws wide, teeth glistening.

"It sounds like a dentist's drill," Shark yells at Dervish, scowling at the noise. "You really like this crap?"

"It's the new wave," Dervish grins. "The music of change. *An-ar-cheeeeeee!*" He punches the air with his fist.

"Grow up," Shark snorts, then looks down at me. "You like this?"

"I've never heard anything like it," I tell him. "It's giving me a headache."

Shark laughs. "The kid's got more sense than you, Grady."

The song ends and the band take a short break so that one of the guitarists can replace the guitar which he's just broken. Dervish uses the lull to fill me in.

"Somebody's summoning a demon. We've been trying to stop him for the last couple of weeks. We don't know who the summoner is, but we know the crossing's going to happen here, tonight. If we can't stop it, we plan to kill the demon or push it back."

"We won't be able to kill it," Shark says. "We're not strong enough to destroy a demon. In the Demonata's universe, maybe — but driving it back is the best we can hope for here."

"Have you done this a lot?" I ask.

"I have. This is Grady's first taste of action." He punches Dervish's arm. "I'm not sure he's up to it."

"Don't worry about me," Dervish growls. "I'll do what I have to."

"I know you will," Shark chuckles. "Now, let's try and find the demon-loving scumbag, though I guess we won't know who it is until—"

"He's over there," I interrupt, pointing at a middle-aged man near the stage. He's dressed like a punk, but doesn't really fit the part. Lean and muscular, with a thick Mohican haircut. His lips are moving steadily. He's the focus for the patches of light. They're pulsing round him in an almost fully formed window.

"How do you know?" Shark asks suspiciously.

"Never mind. That's him. He's almost done. Another few minutes and the window will open."

Shark curses, then starts towards the man with the Mohican. Dervish pushes after Shark, and I head after Dervish. As we're nudging through the crowd, the band howls into a new, faster song and the place goes wild. Suddenly, punks are leaping all around me, bashing into one another, falling over, kicking and punching everyone in sight.

I'm knocked to the floor. Someone stamps on my right hand. I yell with pain. Try to get up, but I'm knocked down again. Struggling, panting, afraid I'm going to be crushed to death by a sea of punks.

Then Shark is beside me, lashing out with his fists, pounding the punks away. Dervish picks me up and gives me a fireman's lift. He's stronger than he looks. "Hold on tight," he says, and we push forward again, Shark clearing a path.

I hit out at a few of the punks, taking advantage of my position, trying to smash a few noses in revenge. Then I remember I've a more important mission and turn my attention to the stage. I have a better view of the demon summoner from here. I see him start to tremble. He froths at the mouth. The lights in the window pulse at the same time.

"Too late!" I shout. "It's going to open."

"No!" Shark roars, shouldering an especially large punk out of his way. "We can make it! I'm not going to—"

An explosion. Part of the stage erupts, showering the people closest to it with splinters and nails. Agonised screams. One of the guitarists falls to his knees, face a pulped, bloody mess. The singer doesn't stop. He's so caught up in his song, he doesn't hear anything except his own voice.

There's a violet coloured window of light next to the Mohican man. He's standing by it proudly, unharmed. He smiles at the chaos. Puts a couple of fingers between his lips and whistles shrilly.

A demon bounds through the window. The body of a large chicken. Three pig-like heads. It looks ridiculous, almost laughable, until it opens a mouth and spits at a nearby punk. The spit hits him squarely in the face, then bubbles and burns his flesh away. He falls, trying to scream, but unable to.

Dervish called for anarchy a few minutes ago — now he gets it. The room was wild with dancing, writhing and fighting before this, but when the punks see the demon in action they go completely mental. Panic sweeps the crowd. Shrieking, they surge for the exit doors. The man with the Mohican laughs and steps up next to the demon.

"Now we'll see who has power!" he shouts over the chaotic screams. "All these years of having to lick somebody else's boots and bow down. No more! Now you'll learn to fear me. This is my world now. All of you—"

He gets no further. The demon, displaying no sense of gratitude, spits at the man. He's flung backwards, the acidic spit already setting to work on his face, dissolving his flesh and cartilage, eating through to sizzle his brain. Who said there was no justice in the world?

We're pushed back and hammered down by the rioting crowd. Shark yells with rage and surprise. He tries fighting them off, but he isn't powerful enough to stand against the tide of panicked punks. I go down again and feel the room close around me. This time I'm certain I'll be crushed.

But Dervish keeps his cool. There's magic in the air — I can feel it seeping through the window. He draws on it, barks a few words and suddenly the space around us is clear, punks wedged aside by an invisible force. The three of us are alone, protected by a bubble of magic energy, like the one Nadia and the others fashioned on top of the needle of rock.

"Shark!" Dervish yells, nodding at the demon, which has spat at a third punk and is now bent over the remains of the man with the Mohican. It's slurping up the spit, along with the gooey mush which is all that's left of the man's skull and brains.

"On it," Shark grunts, stepping forward. He taps into the magic, tenses, then leaps through the air, landing beside the demon. Before it can react, he grabs one of its heads and twists savagely left, then right, ripping it loose.

The demon screeches and spits at Shark with both remaining mouths. Shark ducks out of the way of one of the spitballs and deflects the other with a wave of a magically charged hand. He throws the severed head – still moving – through the window, then grabs for another. This time the demon dodges the tattooed fingers and takes flight, making a noise which is a weird cross between a pig's squeal and a chicken's cluck.

The demon's heading for one of the windows at the front of the building. Before it gets there and breaks through to kill the punks who've spilled out on to the street past the bewildered doormen, Dervish mutters a quick spell. The glass turns to steel. The demon doesn't see this. It leaps, cackling, only to slam hard into the metal and flop to the floor.

Dervish uses magic to clear a path between us and the demon. He darts forward while the demon's shaking its heads with confusion. Gets between the monster and the front door. "Are you sure we can't kill it?" he shouts at Shark.

"Yes!" Shark bellows.

"Then let's force it back through the window." He sneaks a look at me. "Kernel, can you budge over, block its path to the rear doors?"

"I'm not sure," I mutter. "I'm not good at fighting…"

"You won't have to fight," Dervish assures me. "Just look like you know what you're doing, like you're the meanest piece of scum in the room. Scowl. Growl. Howl. If it goes for you, I'll step in."

I trust Dervish, even though I barely know him. He's younger than Shark, but speaks like he's older. So with only the slightest hesitation, I do what he asks and edge my way left, along the path which Dervish is creating. I take up a position halfway between him and Shark, spread my arms, glare at the demon and act as if I'm far more powerful and confident than I feel.

The demon's on its feet. Blood oozes from the neck where its third head was removed. Bile dribbles from its remaining mouths, sizzling where it hits the floor, burning through the old wooden floorboards. It sends a ball of spit zooming at Dervish, but he waves a hand at it and the ball explodes. He chants a spell and several bricks snap loose from the wall and fly at the demon, striking its body and heads.

The demon bats the bricks away, then looks from Dervish to Shark to me. It's searching for a weak point. Its gaze lingers on me, since I'm the smallest. I want to run for cover like the punks, but I don't give in to fear. Instead, I step forward, sneering at the demon, inviting an attack.

The bluff works. With a petulant cry, the demon darts towards the window of violet light, past the singer who's still roaring into his microphone, eyes shut, no idea of what's going on. Shark curses, as though he left the route to the window open by accident. He lunges at the demon. The beast picks up speed, makes it to the window, then leaps to safety, laughing hysterically at Shark, thinking it got the better of him.

"What a team!" Shark hoots, standing to the left of the window, on his guard in case the demon returns. "Did you see that baby run? We kicked its ass royally!"

"What a buzz," Dervish murmurs, closing in on the window, pausing to melt the walls around the front and rear doors, allowing more of the punks to exit — easier than trying to restore order. "I've never felt so powerful. Never knew I could do so much. The magic in the air… the way I tapped into it… unbelievable!"

"You've got the taste for this now," Shark chuckles. "You were nervous earlier. That's understandable. We all get the jitters the first time. But you've caught the bug. It's demon-fighting all the way for you now, right?"

"Maybe," Dervish says, smiling crookedly, looking at his hands with a mix of pride and wonder. "I did most of it without thinking. It was like there was somebody else inside me, pulling the strings."

"The steel windows were a good idea," Shark commends him. "You're more imaginative than me. I'd have tried to drag the demon back."

"How long will the window to the other universe remain open?" Dervish asks.

"Maybe a few minutes," Shark says. "We'll stick by it until it closes, to be safe, then get out of here quick. Try explaining to a policeman that you're part of the great war against demons — see where it gets you!"

Dervish examines the window with innocent curiosity. He pokes his fingers into the light, yelps when they disappear, clutches his hand back and wriggles his fingers, relieved to see them still in place.

Shark laughs. "I did that the first time too."

"Have you ever stepped through?" Dervish asks.

"Once. Came back right away — didn't want to get stuck over there."

"What did you see?"

"A world like ours, only–"

"I have to go," I cut in. They'd forgotten about me. Now they stare. "Beranabus. I've got to get back to him. Remember?"

"You want to step through the window?" Shark frowns.

"No. But I have to. I can find him when I'm in the demon universe."

"What if the monster's waiting for you on the other side?" Dervish says.

I shrug unhappily. "I don't have a choice. I can't find Beranabus here."

"Won't he come for you?" Shark asks.

"Maybe. But I'm not sure he can find me as easily as I can find him. I have to go," I say, urgently this time, aware that the window might close while we're arguing. "A demon stole my brother. I have to rescue him."

I take a step towards the window. Shark puts out a large tattooed hand and stops me. "There's no way I'm going to let a kid walk through that alone," he growls. As my face crumples, he smiles. "So I'd better tag along, make sure you don't come to any harm. Dervish?" He raises a questioning eyebrow.

Dervish studies the window again. Licks his lips nervously. Then nods quickly. "Yeah. What the hell. There's never much to do here on a Saturday anyway."

My eyes fill with happy tears. "Thank you," I mumble.

"Never mind the thanks," Shark sniffs. "Just be ready to fight." And saying that, he grabs the collar of my T-shirt and hurls me through the violet window of light, back into the cauldron of the Demonata.

THE RELUCTANT DISCIPLE

→I come out on top of a fluffy cloud. Through a break to my left I see land far below. My stomach drops as I picture myself falling through the mist, then the sky, hitting the ground hard and splattering. But the cloud holds, supporting me like the water in the first world I visited.

Shark steps through after me, Dervish just behind him. They yell with shock when they see what we're standing on. Turn to dive back through the window. "It's OK!" I shout. "We won't fall."

They pause, glance at me uncertainly, then realise I'm telling the truth — otherwise we'd have already dropped.

The now two-headed demon is on another bank of cloud ahead of us. When it spots us, it squeals with fear and bounds away. Shark starts after it, but Dervish calls him back. "We're here to find Beranabus, not kill a stray demon."

Shark pulls a face, loath to let the demon escape. Then he sighs. "OK, kid. Tell us how you plan to find him."

"I'll open a window," I say, as the one we stepped through comes apart. "Just give me a few minutes to find the patches."

"'Patches'?" Dervish echoes, but I don't answer. Looking around, I'm pleased to note that there are loads of patches of light in the air, despite the fact that we're standing on top of a cloud. I start thinking about Beranabus, muttering his name softly, hoping he's still alive and that I have the power to make the lights pulse.

For a few seconds — nothing. But before panic has a chance to set in, a pink square by my left foot blinks. Then a brown octagon. Soon, dozens of the patches are pulsing and I merrily set to work.

I'm aware of Dervish and Shark talking while I build the window. Dervish is complaining about the cold. His leather jacket is too small to button up properly – it's for style, not warmth – and his bare chest is freezing in these icy heights.

"Use magic," I tell him, recalling the way I instinctively repaired my broken arm. "You can warm up if you think yourself warm."

Dervish is sceptical, but gives it a go, and moments later he's beaming, even taking his jacket off and tying it around his waist.

"You must have been here a long time to know so much," Shark says.

"Actually, I don't think it's been more than half a day," I reply. "Though it feels longer. I'll tell you about it later, if we have time."

The window comes together smoothly under my guidance. I don't hurry. Pleased to note I'm no longer hungry or tired. Marvelling at the way this universe works. I start wondering if we could float down to the ground from here, but then the assembled patches pulse as one and a brownish window opens. "Here we go," I say smugly.

"I didn't think windows could be opened that quickly or simply," Shark says.

"It's easy-peasy when you know how."

Shark steps up beside me and looks back at Dervish. "Ready for the next leg of the tour?"

"Hurm," Dervish says uncertainly. "Do you know where that leads?" he asks me.

"No. But Beranabus will be there." I hesitate. "When I left him, he was in trouble, fighting a team of demons. We might have to help him. So be prepared, OK?"

"Yes, boss," Shark laughs.

"Thanks for warning us," Dervish says, then takes up a position to my left. Shark slides into place on my right. We step through the window.

→It's the same world where Nadia and I ran out on Beranabus. Night. Three moons shine, closer than the moon is to Earth in my universe. Too bright to see if there are any giant demons soaring overhead.

Corpses are scattered across the hard yellow ground. Demons in an advanced state of decomposition, most rotted to the bone. Either demons rot quickly here or this is one of those places where time runs faster than in the human universe.

I spy Beranabus working on a window. Sharmila is nearby, sitting next to a mound of freshly dug earth. I guess it's Raz's final resting place, that she and Beranabus – probably just her – dug a grave for the fallen Disciple.

I get a lump in my throat when I think about how Raz died, but there's no time to cry. I didn't believe I could be so matter of fact about the death of a friend, but I'm learning a lot here. One of the things is that in times of severe disorder, you can't worry about the dead, only the living. I still think Art is alive. He's the one I have to focus on. I can't do any good for the dead Raz Warlo.

"Beranabus!" I call. "It's me, Kernel. I'm back."

The magician's head whips round and Sharmila's jerks up. They stare at me in disbelief, then at the two men with me. Then Beranabus cheers – the first time he's acted like an ordinary human since I met him – and rushes across to pick me up and whirl me around.

"Kernel Fleck!" he booms. "You're a wonder! I've been struggling to build a window to you for days. And here you pop up, cool as a breeze! You're the most remarkable human I've met in centuries!"

He sets me down and I find myself grinning at him. I hadn't liked the cranky magician before. But now I see he can be as emotional as any normal person. He simply hides his feelings better than most.

"Hello, Beranabus," Shark says, stepping forward, hand outstretched.

Beranabus shakes the hand briefly, frowning. Then he points at Shark and says, "Octopus?"

"Shark," Shark laughs.

"Ah. I knew it was something like that." He looks at Dervish blankly.

"This is Dervish Grady," Shark introduces him. "My latest recruit."

"Another Disciple," Beranabus murmurs, nodding shortly at Dervish. "How many does that make?"

"If you don't know, I'm sure nobody does," Shark says.

Beranabus shrugs. "I never was good at numbers. Anyway, welcome to the team, Grady. I hope you last longer than some of my other followers." His eyes flash on Raz's grave.

"It is good to see you again, Kernel," Sharmila says, stepping forward to hug me. She looks drawn and miserable, but has reattached her arm and healed her wounds since the battle.

"I'm pleased you made it," I whisper.

"It was close. My injuries were fatal. If not for Beranabus, I would have died."

"Yes, yes, I'm better than any doctor," Beranabus says impatiently. "Now what about my other Disciple? Where's Nadia? Not dead, surely."

I pause. Part of me wants to cover up for her and tell him she was killed by a demon. But his small dark eyes are fixed on me and I find myself incapable of attempting a lie. "She didn't want to come back. She left me. Went off by herself. She's had enough of demons."

Beranabus's face blackens with fury. "I'll flay her skin from her back! Find her. Open a window to her. Immediately."

"I do not think you should do that," Sharmila says. "Nadia is a free agent. If she wants to—"

"I don't care about her wants!" Beranabus bellows. "We need her. Now open that window, Kernel, and don't pretend you can't. I'll know if you're lying. And I'll punish you for it."

I want to tell him to get stuffed, I'm not his servant. But those dark eyes are fierce with anger when I look at him and I wilt. "I'll try," I mutter unhappily. "I'm not sure it will work, since she's not in this universe, but I'll give it a go. If you're certain."

"Aye!" Beranabus growls, glaring at me as I clear my thoughts and concentrate on Nadia's image, feeling like a traitor of the lowest, meanest order.

→We're waiting for Beranabus. He said that because of the time differences between this world and ours, he could be gone for a few hours as we experience it, even though it will only be a few minutes for him. I keep an eye on the window, holding it open. It's not hard. When I see a patch or two shimmer and start to slip free of the panel, I press them back into place.

We chat to pass the time. Sharmila tells Dervish and Shark about the Kah-Gash, Beranabus's quest, her part in the mission. I describe how I got mixed up in it, and demonstrate how I can construct windows so quickly, though I can't explain why I alone can see the patches of light.

In return, Shark and Dervish tell us of their lives. Shark's been a Disciple for several years, working with others to avert demonic crossings. He was in the army when he discovered his magical talent. On a tour of duty. A village came under attack from four demons. Shark and his team tried to stop them. A Disciple was present. He realised Shark's potential when he saw him fighting, pulled him clear of the massacre, explained about the Demonata. All of Shark's fellow soldiers were killed, so Shark became a Disciple, though he still wears his uniform out of respect for the dead.

Dervish is new to the game. Shark discovered him a few months ago while trying to stop a crossing in the city where I met them. He was successful, thanks to Dervish, who happened to be nearby when a window was about to open. Dervish saw that Shark was in trouble, ran to his aid and used magic he'd never known he possessed to knock out the woman trying to open the window. That was the end of life as he knew it.

"Is that how Disciples are normally recruited?" I ask. "There's an attack, they discover magic within themselves and a Disciple asks them to join?"

"Pretty much," Shark says. "Lots of people have magical ability, but it usually only reveals itself in the presence of demons. When windows are created, some of the magic of their universe flows through, which people like us can tap into, even without training or intent. We've spent decades trying to identify and develop the potential some other way, but no luck so far."

"Does everybody join once they know they have the power?" I ask.

"No," Sharmila answers. "Many reject their calling. I do not blame them. Ours is a harsh life, lonely, filled with peril."

Shark snorts with contempt. "If I had my way, we'd press-gang the lot of them, force them to fight."

"That would be unfair," Sharmila says.

"This isn't about fairness," Shark argues. "It's about winning a war. You can't run away from your duty during war. It's desertion."

"That's what Nadia did," I say softly, and my eyes meet Sharmila's. We're both worried about what will happen when Beranabus catches up with her.

→Nadia falls hard through the window and lands heavily on the ground. She howls hatefully and tries to leap back through the panel of light. Beranabus appears before she completes the jump. Shoves her away, snarling like an animal. "Stop!" he roars.

Nadia tries to wriggle around him, fingers stretching towards the window of light. He blocks her way, standing firm like a Roman emperor, while Nadia shrieks and wails.

She tries using magic to move him, but he flicks aside her bolt of energy and holds his position. "Kernel!" he shouts. "Dismantle the window."

"I'm not sure I should—"

He flashes his teeth at me, making it very clear that he'll turn on me next if I disobey him. Feeling lousy and afraid, I slink around Nadia and Beranabus — the magician fending his assistant off, protecting me from her — and set to the work on the window. After removing a few pieces, the patches slide apart and the window disappears.

Nadia throws herself flat and weeps into the yellow earth, hammering the ground with her fists. Beranabus sighs and steps aside, rubbing the back of his neck. "You'll thank me for this later," he says.

"I'll thank the demon who rips your head off and fills your skull with fire!" she screams back, then bolts upright and glares at me. "*You* showed him where to find me!"

"I had to," I mutter shamefully. "He said he'd—"

She spits at me.

"Do not blame the boy," Sharmila says, putting her hands on my shoulders. "He argued to leave you be, as did I. But Beranabus would not listen."

"Why?" Nadia cries, whirling on Beranabus. "Why didn't you leave me there? I could have been happy. Led a normal life. Been human again. Why rip me away from all that?"

"I need you," Beranabus says flatly.

"No you don't! I gave you what you wanted — a vision which might help you find part of the Kah-Gash."

"There will be other parts to find."

"But that could take hundreds of years! Thousands! We'll both be dead long before that happens — if it ever does."

Beranabus shrugs.

"This is slavery," Nadia snarls. "You always said I was free to leave."

"And you are," Beranabus insists. "As soon as we find the pieces of the Kah-Gash. Until then, I need you. Your universe needs you. I know you don't enjoy this, but that doesn't matter. You've been chosen, like the rest of us. If we turn our backs on our responsibility, the entire world will fall to the Demonata."

"I don't care!" Nadia shrieks. "What's the difference between fighting them here or on my own world? They might as well take it over for all it matters to me!"

"Then you would never have anywhere safe to go," Beranabus says.

"So? I can't go there anyway while you're holding me prisoner."

Beranabus exhales sharply, starts to say something, stops, then smiles tightly. "We'll make a deal. Stay with me until I find this piece of the Kah-Gash. After that, you can go. I'll open a window to the human world for you and not stand in your way."

"And if I die during the search?" Nadia retorts. "Or if it takes a hundred years to find it? Or if you never find it?"

Beranabus's smile disappears. "I'm trying to be reasonable."

Nadia laughs. "No. You know this is wrong and you want to feel better about it. You don't want to admit you're as ruthless and monstrous as the demons you claim to hate."

"I never said I hated the Demonata," Beranabus says quietly. "And I never claimed to be anything other than – as you say – ruthless and monstrous. That's how I need to be to fight them."

Nadia prepares another curse, then realises it would be a waste of breath. She looks around at us, hateful and alone. Points a finger at Beranabus. "You betrayed me. That's something I won't forget or forgive. You don't just have to watch out for demons any more — when I'm around, you'll have to worry about me too. I hate you as much as they do now, and I'll quite gladly kill you if I ever get the chance. And anybody else who's with you."

With that, she turns her back on us, screams at the three moons, then sits and weeps while Beranabus looks on with an unconvincing, half-shameful sneer.

SEARCHING

→An uneasy mood. We're all uncomfortable. Even the gruff Shark, who believes in forcing people to work for the Disciples, isn't used to tyrants like Beranabus.

The magician comes over and sits with us. He scratches the sole of his left foot, then runs a hand through his hair and coughs. "Take no notice of Nadia's hysterics," he says. "She'll be all right when she calms down. We've had similar confrontations before. Although this is the first time she's threatened to kill me." He laughs harshly. Nobody smiles.

"This isn't the best of introductions, is it?" Beranabus notes, looking at me wryly. "You think I'm a heartless beast. But this is the way life is for me. I have no time for decency. I'm a demon killer. That's my sole purpose in life. I sleep soundly – on those rare occasions when I sleep – because I know I'm doing the task that the universe charged me with." He points at my shoes. "You might want to get rid of those. You too, Shark and… Deviant?"

"Dervish."

"Aye. Dump the shoes. They block the flow of magic. Even the slightest advantage can be vital when you're faced with a demon and battling for your life. I'm assuming you two intend to stay and help?"

Shark and Dervish glance at each other edgily. I don't think either *had* planned to stay. Then Shark shrugs and raises an eyebrow. Dervish nods in answer and smiles weakly. They bend to untie their laces.

Beranabus studies me closely as I peel my socks off. "You're a strange one, Kernel Fleck. Normally, I can sense magic in those who possess an abundance of it, but I get almost nothing from you, even though you must be throbbing with power to open windows between worlds so swiftly."

"I don't think it's magic," I say shyly. "It's like a puzzle. I see lights and I'm able to slot them together when they pulse. That's the only difference between me and you. I can see the pieces of the window. You can't."

"Tell me about these lights," Beranabus says. "When you first noticed them and realised you could manipulate them."

"I've seen the lights all my life, but it was only on the needle of rock that I realised I could..." A memory kicks in and I come to a surprised stop. "No, that's not right. A year ago, I put lights together in my bedroom, stepped through the window and went missing for a few days." I can't believe I hadn't remembered that until now.

"*Missing?*" Beranabus sniffs.

"Yes. Nobody knew where I was. I don't know either. I can't remember what happened when I stepped through the window."

"Nothing at all?" Beranabus presses.

I think hard, but even though I now know that I must have crossed into this universe, my mind's a total blank. There's something about the window itself, before I stepped through, but the memory evades me. I shake my head.

Sharmilla has been listening closely. She looks at Beranabus, troubled. "Does it not strike you as strange that of all the places Cadaver could have emerged, he turned up in that village? The home of the one boy in all the world who has a power which in some ways is greater than even your own?"

"You think he went there for Kernel?" Beranabus frowns.

"Perhaps. When we turned up, maybe he thought we were protecting Kernel. So he took the brother instead, gambling that Kernel would chase after him."

"A trap," Beranabus says, nodding slowly. "Aye, it could be. Maybe we should forget about Cadaver and–"

"No!" I hiss. "Art's the only thing in this universe I'm interested in. I don't care if it's a trap — I'm going to keep looking for him. Whether you help me or not. I know how now. I'll use a window to find him."

Beranabus smiles icily. "You could have done that as soon as you returned. But you didn't. Instead you searched for me. Because you need me to snatch your brother back. You can find him, but you can't fight for him. You want me to risk everything I have — for *you*. Do you expect me to do that without asking for anything in return?"

I glower at the magician, but what he says is true. I *am* asking him to risk his life to help me.

"I thought you had to search for this Cadaver demon anyway," Dervish says. "He's the one who can lead you to the weapon, right?"

"Perhaps not directly," Beranabus says. "Nadia's vision wasn't clear. She said the demon thief could guide us. But perhaps he's already done that."

"You think part of the Kah-Gash is here?" Sharmila asks, dubiously looking around at the yellowish demon world.

"No. I think Cadaver was only meant to provide us with the *means* of finding it." He fixes his gaze on me. "*You're* the true guide. Cadaver's role was to lead us to you. Now that we know about your talent, we can use it to search for the Kah-Gash. That's the deal — help me locate the fragments, then I'll help you get your brother back."

I stare at Beranabus nervously. It sounds like a fair trade, but I'm wary. Afraid of ending up like Nadia, a tool in the magician's hands, a slave. Nobody knows how many pieces the Kah-Gash was broken up into. It could be a handful or it could be a thousand.

"Help me rescue Art now," I barter. "Then I'll search for the weapon."

Beranabus shakes his head. "The Kah-Gash first. You won't have any reason to help me once you have your brother back. You could open a window and slip away from me any time you wished."

I think it over carefully, not wanting to tie myself to a deal which might backfire on me later. I've never had to bargain like this before. It's strange. Confusing. Frightening. But I force myself to concentrate and think all the options through.

"One piece," I say quietly. "I'll help you search for it. Then we go after Cadaver and Art. That's fair."

Beranabus scowls and starts to argue.

"He is right," Sharmila heads him off. "That is an equal exchange. An eye for an eye, so to speak."

Beranabus makes a grumbling sound. "It's not equal. That's like me saying I'll help you rescue one of your brother's legs. You want the whole boy — well, I want the whole Kah-Gash."

"But I could spend the rest of my life looking for all the pieces!" I cry.

Beranabus rolls his eyes. "Very well," he says reluctantly. "Find the first piece. Then we rescue your brother. Then you help me find the rest of it."

"No!" Sharmila snaps. "You can't ask that of him."

"I can and I did," Beranabus retorts without taking his eyes off me. "Of course, I can't hold you to that promise, but I'll trust you to keep your word if you give it."

I hesitate. My gaze slides to Nadia, still sitting with her back to us, crying. To spend years here like she has, fighting demons, never return home... Do I love Art that much? Would I sacrifice all that I have to save him?

"It may not take as long as you think," Beranabus says. "There might only be a few pieces of the Kah-Gash. Maybe we'll find them within weeks or months. Once I have the weapon, I'll be able to destroy the demon universe. You can go home. Lead a normal, happy, human life."

I nod slowly, deciding. "OK." Beranabus breaks into a smile. "But you've got to agree to help me even if I can't find the Kah-Gash."

The magician's smile vanishes. "Why wouldn't you be able to find it?"

"I don't know if I can search for objects. Maybe I can only open windows to people or demons. If I can find it, I will. But if I search and I can't, I want your word that you'll still help me."

Beranabus considers that. "Very well."

Solemnly, seriously, we shake on the deal. And I try hard not to think about the legend of Faust.

→I move apart from the others. Study the patches of light, all sorts of sizes, shapes and colours. I try not to dwell on the deal. I have to put Art's needs before my own, then hope for the best later.

And if you have to spend the rest of your life in servitude to Beranabus? a voice says within me.

I can't worry about that now. What will be, will be. Art first — after the Kah-Gash.

I'm not sure how to look for it, since I've no idea what exactly it is that I'm searching for. I run the name through my thoughts, studying the lights, hoping some will pulse. But they don't.

I clear my thoughts and try another approach. I think about an object — a tree that I used to climb when I lived in the city. Dozens of lights pulse. I let the image of the tree fade, wait for the lights to return to normal, then experiment again, this time trying to think of an object I'm not familiar with.

It's not as easy as it sounds. I think of famous buildings, cities, Mount Everest. But while I haven't been to those places, I have an image of each inside my head, and when that image pops up, the lights start pulsing.

"Tell me the names of some strange places or things that I won't know about," I say to Beranabus and the others.

"Why?" Beranabus asks.

"Just do it. Please. It's important."

"The Taj Mahal," Sharmila says.

"No. I've seen pictures of that."

"My bedroom," Dervish says with a laugh.

"No. Something specific, with a unique name."

There's a pause, then Beranabus says softly, "Newgrange."

"Perfect!" I haven't the slightest idea what that means. Focusing on the word, I stare at the lights and murmur,

"Newgrange, Newgrange, Newgrange." I keep repeating it, mind blank of images, having only the name to work with.

Several lights pulse, then others, and more drift towards me from points further away. I slot the patches together. When a deep blue window forms, I ask Beranabus to step through with me.

"Why are we going to Newgrange?" he asks.

"I'm testing my powers."

As soon as we emerge, I know we're back in the real world. It's a grey, wet day. Ahead of us stands a strange structure, a long, white brick wall with a doorway in it, a grass mound for a roof.

"Is that Newgrange?" I ask.

"Aye," Beranabus says, a soft smile on his lips. "It was built by the Old Creatures, beings of amazing magic. They kept this world safe from the Demonata for thousands of years. When they moved on, their power passed with them, leaving us open to attacks. I resented their passing when I was younger, but now I think they had to leave, that humans have a destiny of their own, which they must follow by themselves."

I don't really understand that, but it doesn't matter. What I know is that I can use the lights to search for objects which I'm not familiar with. Armed with that knowledge, I retreat through the window, to search once again for the mysterious Kah-Gash.

* * *

→I spend several minutes running the word through my thoughts, but the lights don't respond. Not even a shimmer.

"Does the weapon have another name?" I ask Beranabus.

"Possibly. Demons speak many languages. But most refer to it as the Kah-Gash."

I try for maybe a quarter of an hour, then give up. "It's no good. I can't find it. Either it doesn't exist or I'm not able to locate it without further information."

Beranabus's face darkens. "If you're trying to play me for a fool..."

"I'm not. The lights aren't pulsing. I've tried my hardest, but nothing's happening."

"Maybe you need to give it more time," Beranabus suggests.

"That's not how it worked with the other windows. If I could find your weapon, the lights would have started pulsing by now. I can't do it."

Beranabus mutters something to himself and tugs irritably at his beard.

Sharmila is looking at me, head cocked, frowning. She starts to say something, then changes her mind and instead says, "We must search for Cadaver again."

"To rescue the child?" Beranabus sneers.

"Yes. But also to question the demon. Perhaps he knows another word for the Kah-Gash, which will enable Kernel to locate it."

"Or maybe Nadia was wrong," Beranabus says, glaring at his assistant's back. "Maybe this is a wild goose chase."

Sharmila shrugs. "Perhaps. But if we are to continue, it seems logical to make Cadaver our target."

Beranabus thinks it over, then pins his gaze on me. "Look at me directly and tell me you can't find the Kah-Gash."

I don't like him calling me a liar, but I let our eyes meet and say, "I searched for it honestly. I couldn't find it." I hold his gaze, trying not to blink.

Beranabus scowls. "Very well. We'll pick up Cadaver's trail and hope he hasn't laid any more traps for us. Go ahead then, boy. Find him."

"First, you have to promise to help me rescue Art."

"Don't worry," Beranabus huffs. "We'll do all we can to save your little brother. If he's still alive." He spits spitefully. "Which I very much doubt."

HELL-CHILD

→I don't search for Cadaver directly, figuring that wherever Art is, the demon must be too. (*Unless he killed Art and dumped his body as he darted between worlds*, says an inner voice which I ignore.) So I search for my brother instead. To my surprise, it takes me a few seconds to bring up an image of him. His face is hazy in my mind and I have to concentrate hard to make it clear. For some odd reason, I think of the orange marbles which he was playing with before he was stolen. He dropped them on his way to the window and I picked them up. Put them in my pocket. I reach in and touch them now, and when I do that, I click on an image of Art in Sally's house, that night in the bedroom when he was holding them up in front of his eyes.

As soon as I recall that, a number of lights round me pulse. Many are orange, reminding me of the orange patch I saw over Art's head that time. Maybe individual colours are associated with certain people. I must take more notice of the colours the next time I'm looking for someone, to check.

I haven't reached out to the lights yet. I find myself reluctant to start. Afraid almost. Because now, finally, I have to face the facts. If Art's dead, I'll know as soon as I step through the window. I've been living in hope, trying to convince myself that he's alive and well. But once I put these pulsing lights together, hope will vanish, leaving me with the truth. Which is fine if Cadaver hasn't killed him. But if he has...

I steel myself against the possible awfulness of the discovery. I can't falter now, when I'm so close. If I'd known about my gift earlier, I could have gone after him from that first demon world. But this has been a learning process. I've found out things about myself, and this strange universe, bit by bit. Time to put my learning to good use — and pray it's not too late.

I let out a deep breath. Scratch an itchy spot on my head. Start to slot the lights into place.

→The window is orange when it forms, which is no great surprise. I step back from it, nervous, thinking about how angry Beranabus will be if Art isn't with Cadaver.

The magician steps up to the window and sniffs at it. Looks back at us. There's a glint to his eyes which, looking round, I see reflected in Shark's. The eager glint of men who enjoy fighting. Sharmila looks scared. Dervish seems more confused than anything else. He's put his leather jacket on and is stroking one of his spiky clumps of hair for comfort.

"Nadia," Beranabus calls. She's still sitting with her back to us, though her shoulders are no longer heaving. At the call, she stands and turns. Her pale, pockmarked face is composed, like a mask. Her eyes are red from crying but there are no fresh tears. She walks towards us at an even pace, stops close to Beranabus, looks at him without interest.

"I want you to concentrate," Beranabus says. "See if you can gain an insight which might let us know what's on the other side."

Nadia smiles coldly. "I'm not feeling very insightful," she says then steps through the window before Beranabus can respond.

Beranabus curses, but the slightest look of guilt flits across his face. He shrugs it off and nods sharply at Sharmila. "You next. I'll come after you. Then the boy, Dervish and Shark. Is everybody ready?"

"Ready for what?" Dervish asks.

Beranabus chuckles. "*Hell*, most likely."

→Webs everywhere. Strand after strand, some the thickness of several trees placed together, others as fine as a length of thread. A gloomy, silvery, moonless sky, dotted with giant meteor-like demons. Nothing but blackness when I look down through the many layers of web. I wriggle my bare toes over the moist, sticky fabric of the strand. It's like standing on candyfloss.

There's a demon close to us, a nightmarish beast. He has the body of a child but the head of an adult. Pale green skin.

No hair, but a wig-like cluster of lice scuttle around his scalp, feeding on his flesh, digging holes through to his brain. No eyes —instead, a ball of fire burns in either socket. A large mouth full of sharp teeth, no tongue. Two smaller mouths set in his palms, one in either hand.

The demon hisses when he sees us, turns and races away at a great speed, crisscrossing the network of webs, leaping from one level to another. Nobody gives chase, not even Shark. We've just spotted the castle towards which the demon is running.

A castle of webs, set amidst a cluster of extra thick strands. It looks like a medieval castle, except ten times bigger. Taller than any skyscraper I've ever seen, wider than a couple of street blocks in the city where I used to live. Towers and turrets galore. Several huge drawbridges. Everything spun out of webs. Glistening and forbidding, even from this distance.

There's a moat round the castle. The hell-child leaps across it with ease, but instead of waiting for the drawbridge to be lowered, he scales the outside wall of the castle like a spider. Disappears through a narrow window.

"This is bad," Beranabus says.

"You know this place?" Sharmila asks.

"It's the home of a demon master called Lord Loss."

"I like his style," Shark grunts, then looks around. "So, where's the demon we're meant to be chasing?"

"Where else?" Beranabus points to the castle.

"How do you know?" Dervish asks.

"No demon can set foot here without Lord Loss's permission. Only his familiars and those he chooses to shelter are welcome. Cadaver isn't one of his slaves, so I'm guessing he asked for sanctuary and it was granted — otherwise he would have fled from here already."

"Company's coming," Nadia says, smirking at us crookedly.

I spot scores of demons wriggling through the windows of the castle and over the tops of turrets. A couple of the drawbridges are lowered and more of the monsters advance over them.

Dervish glances back at the orange window, still open behind us. He looks at Beranabus questioningly.

"No," the magician says after a moment's hesitation. "We can't defeat Lord Loss on his own territory. But maybe we can bargain with him."

"Bargain with a demon?" Sharmila frowns.

"He's not like other demons. He prefers suffering to execution — he feeds on the misery of the living rather than the bodies of the dead. He won't kill us swiftly. If we can find some way to amuse him... give him something which Cadaver can't... maybe he'll turn the thief over to us. And let us go."

"You really believe that?" Sharmila asks.

"No," Beranabus chuckles drily. "But it's the only hope we have."

Then the demons are upon us.

FLY ON THE WALL

→Fighting desperately. Swamped by demons of every mutation imaginable. Some are small, like the one we saw when we arrived. Others tower above us. Many are strange hybrids — mixtures of animals, lizards, birds, even fish. Others look like nothing I've ever seen, lumps and blobs, teeth and claws, shadows and blood.

We fight in a tight circle, back to back. Sharmila sets the demons on fire when they come within reach. Shark rips heads and limbs loose, using the severed arms and legs as clubs to beat back other demons — he's loving this. Dervish uses bolts of magical energy where he can, his fists and feet when a demon closes in. Nadia has magically grown her nails and is using them as swords, ten deadly blades. Beranabus uses a mix of spells and punches to shatter the bodies of our enemies, fighting calmly, controlled.

I lash out with my fists, punching wildly, trying to be as much of a nuisance as possible. I'm not terrified. Scared, but in control. Panting hard, but not roaring. Maybe it's because

I know this is a fight which can't be avoided. Even if I ran away, I'd have to come back and face these demons again. Unless I abandon Art. Which isn't going to happen.

The demons should have overwhelmed us by now. There are so many of different sizes, shapes and powers. We shouldn't be able to stand up to them. But they don't take advantage of their strength and numbers. They snap and bite at us, inflicting minor wounds, but don't pile upon us all at once.

"What's going on?" Dervish yells, wiping a demon's yellow blood from his face and kicking an otter-like beast away. "Why are we still alive?"

"Like I said," Beranabus grunts, "Lord Loss wants to play. He must have given orders not to kill us."

"Then why don't we stop fighting?" Dervish asks.

"When demons catch the scent of blood, they don't always obey their master's orders," Beranabus chuckles.

"So are we just going to stay here?" Sharmila shouts, face bright, lit by the flames of the burning demons around her.

"No," Beranabus says. "Let's move towards the castle. But keep up our defences. I think they'll let us through, but they won't make it easy for us. If one of us stumbles and falls behind..."

He doesn't finish. Doesn't need to. It's clear that anyone who stumbles will be left for the demons.

*　　*　　*

→Battling our way through the ranks of demons, edging across the strands of web, feet sticky, coated with a glue-like substance. The stench is unbelievable — not just the demons, but all the blood and guts. The webs around us are slick with the entrails and life juices of the demons we've wounded or killed. Lord Loss must be a strange master to let so many of his servants perish at our hands.

Some of the wounded fall between the layers of webs and disappear into the darkness, howling and screaming. But their cries never last more than a few seconds. As we draw close to the moat, and pass over a patch where the webby strands are thin and sparse, I see what happens to those who fall.

There are shark-like demons floating in the darkness beneath the layers of webs, constantly circling. Whenever a demon falls, the sharks move in for the kill, ripping the unfortunate monster to shreds, sometimes swallowing it whole.

In this universe, just when you think things can't get any worse, they usually do!

→We come to a halt at the edge of the moat. This close, I see that it's actually just open space — a circular gap between the layers of web, with nothing to stop us falling straight down to where the shark demons are waiting. The bridges have been drawn closed, leaving us with no simple way of getting across.

As I'm staring at the webby castle walls with one eye, keeping the other on the demons, I get the strangest sense of déjà vu, like I've seen this place before. But I can't have. I'm probably just thinking about castles I've seen in books and movies.

A demon with powerful hind legs bounces high into the air and throws itself at Dervish while he's grappling with another of the beasts. Acting on instinct, the punk lowers his head and the spikes of his hair turn to steel. The demon is impaled and dies screaming. Dervish flicks his head left, then right, dislodging the dead demon. He bellows at Beranabus, "What now?"

"We have to jump across and scale the wall," Beranabus shouts.

"I don't think I can jump that far," I roar.

"Then we'll leave you behind for the Demonata," Beranabus retorts. Before I can think of a reply, the magician grabs the back of my neck and leaps. A second of stomach-dropping terror as I gaze down into the abyss and the circling shark demons. Then we hit the wall and stick. "Come on!" Beranabus yells at the others.

Shark jumps with ease. So does Nadia. Dervish is nervous and flails with his arms when jumping, but he makes it. Just as Sharmila leaps, a demon snags her sari. She rips free, but the attack robs her of her momentum, and instead of sailing across the moat, she falls towards the sharks.

"No!" Dervish shouts, reaching for her — but he's too late. He misses. She falls. I open my mouth to scream.

Then Beranabus is beside her. He wraps an arm around her. Angles her upwards. Soars back to the wall with her, holding on until she gets a grip on the webs. She's sobbing weakly — she thought she was finished.

"You never told us you could fly," Shark grunts.

"It varies from world to world," Beranabus says. "In some I can. In others I can't."

"Did you know you could fly here?" Dervish asks.

Beranabus shrugs. "I had a pretty good idea."

Which means he wasn't sure. He risked his life when he threw himself after Sharmila. Another sign that he isn't as cold and unfeeling as he pretends.

As we're clinging to the wall, the drawbridge nearest us is lowered. It's amazing how it operates — the bridge and the mechanism driving it are constructed entirely of webs. Even in the middle of my fear and madness I pause and mutter, "Cool!"

There's no creaking sound as the drawbridge touches down on the other side of the moat. Perfect silence. The demons have stopped chattering and howling. All are focused on the drawbridge now, holding their position, waiting for... what?

We soon find out.

I spy the shadow of something small, coming out of the castle. At first, I think it's the lice-headed, fire-eyed demon we saw when we arrived, but then the figure comes into sight and my heart gives an actual physical leap.

"*Art!*" I scream as my kidnapped brother totters on to the drawbridge. He looks at me and giggles. Exactly as I remembered him. Unharmed by the demons. Not the least bit afraid. Looks as happy and at home as he did in Paskinston.

My initial urge is to rush to my brother, but Beranabus snaps, "Stay where you are!"

"But it's—"

"I know. But wait. Let's see what comes out after him."

As he says it, I see two more shadows appear. The first of the pair steps out. It's Cadaver, the demon thief, looking as hairy and loathsome as the last time I saw him. His long ears are upright and his wide, white eyes are alert. He picks up Art and glares at us with his half-human, half-canine face. Art cuddles up to the demon and a bolt of jealousy shoots through me.

Then the other figure appears and jealousy washes away to be replaced by awe and terror — and recognition.

The creature is maybe seven or eight feet tall. He has eight arms, each of which ends in stubby, misshapen fingers, with bones sticking out of the flesh. No legs or feet, just long strips of flesh beneath the waist. He doesn't touch the floor of the drawbridge, but hovers in the air. Lumpy skin, a pale red shade, cracked in dozens of places, blood oozing from the cracks. Bald like me. Dark red eyes, no white at all. A small mouth with a grey tongue and teeth. No nose, just two holes set above his upper lip. A gaping hole in the left side of his chest, where his heart should be. Lots of small snakes inside the hole, wriggling around, hissing and spitting.

This was what I was trying to remember earlier, when Beranabus was asking me about the first window I formed, a year ago, when I went missing. Just before I stepped through, something looked out at me from the other side. It was a demon. *This* demon.

He's one of the creepiest monsters I've seen, but that's not what sets him apart. He has an air of authority. I can feel the menace, the evil, the energy and power. Easy to see why these other demons obey him, why they stand like soldiers in the presence of a general, awaiting his command, eager to please him, afraid of what he'll do if he loses his temper.

This is a demon of an entirely different class. I can sense it. So can the others. Even Shark doesn't look confident any longer. I know now why Beranabus doesn't want to fight this monster. Why he said we couldn't.

It's Lord Loss. It must be. It couldn't be anybody else.

→After several seconds of silence, which I'm sure Lord Loss allows just so we can admire his awful beauty, the demon master reaches out with one of his eight hands and pats Art on the head. Art gurgles and tries to bite into the bloodstained flesh. Lord Loss jerks his hand away before Art brings his teeth together — even demon masters are wary of my little biter of a brother!

Lord Loss's head turns right, slowly. Fresh cracks open around his neck and shoulders. Blood flows from them. He levels his gaze on us, studying us one at a time. Nadia is murmuring the words of some spell — a protective spell perhaps, though I don't think that will be much use if he decides to attack. Lord Loss observes her longer than the rest of us, frowning softly, then his eyes move on.

As he studies me, I remember how he looked at me before, the way his eyes lingered on me then, how I stood up to him. He could have crossed that night, I'm sure, and taken me. But I stared him down. Made a fist and threatened him with magic. He wasn't sure how powerful I was. He retreated. That gives me hope and the strength to look at him directly now, without flinching.

"It is pleasing to see you again after all these years, Beranabus," Lord Loss finally says, breaking the heavy silence. His voice is the saddest I've ever heard, as if everyone close to him had recently died in tragic, painful circumstances.

"I don't know if I would call it a pleasure exactly," Beranabus answers.

"This is the first time you have visited me here, though I have felt you pass a few times before. You should not have waited so long, old friend."

"I'd have happily waited a few more centuries."

The pair smile thinly at each other. I can tell there's no love lost between them. If we survive, I must ask Beranabus to tell me about their history. I bet it's an interesting story.

Lord Loss lets his gaze settle on me again. He sighs mournfully. "Cornelius Fleck. I hoped you would not embark on such a foolhardy quest. You should have stayed and comforted your father and mother. They are distraught without you, even after all this time. I know you love your brother, but it would—"

"What do you mean?" I interrupt, curiosity forcing me to speak. "It's only been a few days since I left home."

The demon master makes a miserable sound. "You poor child. Did Beranabus not explain the vagaries of time in this universe?"

"Yes," I say uneasily. "But... I mean... a couple of days... it can't make much of a..." I look to Beranabus. "How long *have* I been here?"

"I don't know," he says shiftily. "It doesn't matter."

"Of course it matters," Lord Loss disagrees. "The boy thinks he can come here, rescue his brother, return and all will be well. If only it were that simple." He sighs again. "I cannot be accurate, Cornelius, since it is hard to judge the passage of time in your universe, but it has been at least five or six years since Cadaver made off with young Art."

"No!" I cry. "That's impossible!"

"I'm afraid it is not only possible — it is true," Lord Loss insists. "You were unfortunate with the worlds you visited, although it may not have been mere misfortune. Cadaver is roguish. He might have chosen those worlds deliberately."

My heart's pounding. Five or six *years*! All the children my age who I knew in Paskinston will be adults now. Mum and Dad must think we're both dead. They'll have grieved and moved on with their lives. If I return with Art, the pair of us looking no older than we did on the day we disappeared...

"Don't think about it," Dervish hisses. "He's probably lying. He wants to destroy your confidence."

"I am not in the habit of lying!" Lord Loss booms, just the slightest hint of anger in his otherwise morbid tone. "In fact, I have never told a lie, have I, Beranabus?"

"So it's said," Beranabus mutters.

"Whatever," Dervish sniffs.

"Dervish is right." Sharmila smiles at me. "Do not think about it. There is a price to pay for coming into this universe. If it is the loss of five or six years... what of it? The important thing is that we return with your brother. Yes?"

"I guess so," I mumble unhappily. "But—"

"Don't start with 'buts'," Dervish warns me. "You'll be 'butting' all night if you do." He squints up at the silvery sky. "If they have nights here."

Lord Loss watches me, a malicious twinkle in his red eyes. As he's studying me, the demons on the other side of the moat begin to fidget and mutter. They're growing impatient. Lord Loss throws a cold glance at them. "I think it will be better if we continue our discussions inside. Less distractions, hmmm?"

Beranabus tenses. "Do I have your word that no harm will befall us in there?"

"I promise that I will not injure you – or allow anyone else to – while we are discussing whatever it is that brought you here. Once those discussions have concluded..." He grins like a corpse.

"We could make a sneak attack, grab Cadaver and the child," Shark whispers. "Kernel could open a window for us."

"Not quickly enough," Beranabus murmurs. "If we anger Lord Loss, and he sets his familiars on us, with orders to kill..." He looks at the ranks of demons. Shakes his head. "Very well," he says to Lord Loss. "We accept your generous offer, with many thanks but no sense of obligation."

Lord Loss nods slowly, then turns and glides back into his castle, Cadaver hurrying ahead of him with Art, perhaps afraid we'll hurl ourselves at him once the demon master's back is turned.

Beranabus crawls towards the drawbridge, cutting across the vertical wall of the castle. I'm reminded of a scene in a Dracula film I saw once. If only vampires were all I had to worry about!

Sharmila is next to cross, followed by Dervish, then Nadia, still softly chanting the words of a spell. Shark motions for me to go ahead, covering my back, in case any of the demons on the other side of the moat attack. I smile my thanks, take one last look at the turrets and towers of the castle, trying to recall why they look so familiar. Then I focus on the drawbridge and drag my way across the wall of webs towards my meeting with the terrible monster who rules within.

AT HOME WITH LORD LOSS

→We trail from one enormous room to another. The rooms are so cavernous, I feel like an ant. The ceilings are all high overhead (a few don't even have ceilings, but open up to the sky), the walls so far apart that you could fit a couple of good-sized houses between them. There's not much in the way of furniture or fittings, but the few pieces I spot — chairs, a statue, a dry fountain — are all made of webs.

It's hot inside and gets hotter the further in we move. I'm soon sweating through my T-shirt. The others are uncomfortable too, pulling at their clothes, trying to breathe more freely. Dervish removes his jacket again, starts to tie it round his waist, then just dumps it. His spikes are drooping from the heat.

Lord Loss doesn't look back. Glides silently, smoothly, following after Cadaver and Art. It's hard to contain myself. I want to dash ahead of the demon master and grab my brother. But I can't. This is Lord Loss's home. I have to respect his rules. I'm not sure what he'd do to me if I didn't, but I'm certain it wouldn't be pleasant.

We enter a room filled with chess sets perched on webby pillars. Ordinary sets, like you'd find in any toyshop. The pieces in different positions on the various boards, as if games were being played on them before we arrived.

Dervish freezes when he sees the chess sets. He takes a few steps away from the rest of us, staring around the room. Then looks at Lord Loss with an entirely new expression. "*You!*" he croaks. "I know you now. You're the one who..."

"Yes," Lord Loss says, pausing to look back. "I knew you were a Grady as soon as I smelt you. The stench of your family cannot be disguised. But I didn't wish to announce myself, in case you had not heard of me."

Dervish is trembling. He starts to say something but Beranabus cuts in. "This is not the time to have a discussion about your family's curse."

"You know about the curse?" Dervish says sharply.

"Evidently."

"And you know about...?" He nods at Lord Loss.

"I'd heard the rumours."

The rest of us look at each other blankly, no idea what this is about. Only Nadia pays no attention, still muttering her spell, gaze fixed on Lord Loss.

"We could play a game if you wish," Lord Loss says eagerly. "A practice match. A chance for us to test each other, in case we ever have to play for real."

Dervish glances at the chess boards, then shakes his head. "That will never happen. I won't have children. I refuse to subject them to the curse, to have them live in fear as I have."

"Noble intentions," Lord Loss murmurs. "But one should not tempt fate by saying never. Perhaps circumstances will conspire against you. Maybe your brother will reproduce..."

"If Cal has kids, he'll account for them himself," Dervish says stiffly.

Lord Loss inclines his head slightly, turns and carries on, further into the castle, out of the room of chess sets. We follow, Dervish visibly shaken, looking over his shoulder at the boards like a man who's seen a ghost.

→We come to a room even larger than the rest. A huge spider-shaped throne in the centre, made of webs. A chandelier overhead, again woven from webs, with naked flames flickering in place of candles or light bulbs. Objects from my world are strewn across the floor — items of clothing, a tennis ball, walking sticks, the skeleton of some large animal, toys, more chess sets, scattered bones. A portrait of Lord Loss on the wall behind the throne, painted in the style of Vincent Van Gogh.

Lord Loss glides to the throne, over the legs which jut out of its base, up to the seat which is set in the body of the spider. He lowers himself on to it, so he can look down on us like a king upon his subjects. Cadaver sits on one of the legs to the left of the throne, playing with Art, holding him up on his knees, then letting him drop and catching him.

The demon master raises a hand to stop us about ten or twelve feet away from the throne. Smiles imperiously, then waves the hand at the room in general. "What do you think of my humble abode?"

"Not what I'd choose," Beranabus says. He nods at some of the objects on the floor. "The remains of previous guests?"

"Mementoes," Lord Loss says. He gestures at a knife, which rises from the floor and floats into his mangled hand. It's not like the knives in our kitchen at home — this is more of a small sword. Lord Loss turns it around a few times, smiling at Beranabus. "You should recognise this. It was yours once."

Beranabus's face is stone. "I'm not interested in the past or your mementoes."

Lord Loss shrugs and lets the knife drop. Art grabs for it, but Cadaver flicks it away before my brother can do any damage with the blade.

"Tell me what you *are* interested in," Lord Loss says. "Tell me why you have come and risked my wrath. You know uninvited visitors are not welcome, that I am entitled to kill you all if I wish — and probably will."

He waves at the walls. Looking up, I see the demons from outside sneaking into the room through windows which I hadn't noticed before. They cling to the walls, growing in number by the second, completely surrounding us. Several block the doorway through which we entered.

"I've been in more promising situations," Shark mutters wryly.

"Do you think we could blast through the walls?" Dervish asks. "They're only webs."

"Magical webs," Sharmila corrects him. "Built to protect Lord Loss from all the demons of this universe. I would not bet on us being able to force a way through."

Beranabus ignores the demons. He's gazing calmly at Lord Loss. Points at Cadaver and says, "We want him."

"The baby?" Lord Loss smiles, misinterpreting the gesture.

"No. The demon."

Lord Loss frowns. He'd expected Beranabus to ask for Art. I had too. I want to yell at the magician and remind him of his promise. But that would be the wrong thing to do. We're in a dangerous spot, the odds stacked against us. I have to trust Beranabus for now. Let him play it the way he wants. Only step in if I feel I absolutely have to.

"Cadaver isn't one of your familiars," Beranabus says. "You're not bound to protect him. I know you've granted him shelter, but I ask you to revoke that privilege and let us take him. We have no quarrel with you. Give us Cadaver and we'll leave at once, owing you a debt which we shall do our best to repay."

"You would put yourself in debt to me?" Lord Loss says, eyes burning bright.

"Yes."

"Tempting," the demon master purrs. "Cadaver must be very important to you. But why? He is an average, unremarkable demon." Lord Loss doesn't know about our quest to find the Kah-Gash so this makes no sense to him.

"Our reasons are private and should be of no concern to you," Beranabus says. "Just as it's no concern of ours why you offered him sanctuary in the first place."

"But that is no secret," Lord Loss laughs. "I gave him shelter because he did a service for me. He brought me the child." Lord Loss glances down at Art, then looks at me mockingly. I know in that instant that Lord Loss gave the order for my brother to be kidnapped. It was no accident that Cadaver took Art — the demon had been searching for him!

Beranabus sees this too. He starts to ask about it then changes his mind. Perhaps he's afraid that Lord Loss will realise he's searching for the Kah-Gash. I don't think the demon master would be so playful if he knew we were after a weapon which could destroy him and every other demon.

"So Cadaver did a service for you, and you rewarded him or promised to," Beranabus says. "Does that make him one of your familiars?"

"No," Lord Loss says and Cadaver looks at him quickly, worried. "But it would be wrong of me to dismiss him. I cannot let you kill him, not until I pay him for his service and he takes his leave. And that could be quite some time — he is under no obligation to depart before he wishes."

"What if we promised not to kill him?" Beranabus presses. "If we only made enquiries of him? I'm not saying we won't harm him, but I'll give my word that he won't die."

The hairs on Cadaver's arms lengthen menacingly and he whines softly. (Again I find myself wondering how he makes any noise, since he doesn't have a mouth.) He holds Art more tightly to his chest, issuing a warning.

"Do not be foolish, my swift-footed friend," Lord Loss says without warmth. "If you harm the child, your torment will be eternal." Cadaver scowls but relaxes his grip. Lord Loss faces Beranabus again, but only after staring at Nadia for a moment. Her lips haven't stopped moving. Maybe he thinks her spell is something we've worked on, that she's part of a trap.

"As tempting as it is, the favour is not enough," Lord Loss says. "I would need a stronger reason to turn Cadaver over to you."

"Such as?" Beranabus asks tightly.

Lord Loss frowns thoughtfully, but it's a deceptive frown — he knows exactly what he's going to ask for. "There is no point in your promising not to kill Cadaver, since it is a promise you cannot guarantee. If I gave him to you, it would have to be unconditionally."

"That suits me fine," Beranabus growls.

Cadaver gets to his feet, trembling with rage and fear. Lord Loss ignores him.

"A life for a life," the demon master whispers. "I will give you Cadaver if you give me one of your followers."

"Which one?" Beranabus asks without blinking. Shark, Sharmila, Dervish and I gawp at him, unable to believe that he'd sacrifice one of us so casually.

"The choice would be mine," Lord Loss murmurs. "All I guarantee is that it won't be you. Otherwise, no deal and I'll unleash my familiars immediately, with orders to slaughter you all."

Beranabus looks around at us. His gaze is steady but there's a slight tremble in his left hand, the only sign that he's not as calm as he seems. Shark returns the stare honestly — he's ready to die if the choice goes against him. But Sharmila, Dervish and I look away. Not that it matters whether we agree or not — the choice is Beranabus's, not ours.

Nadia has stopped chanting. She's sneering at Beranabus. "Go on," she says witheringly. "Don't pretend there's any doubt. Sell us out. It's what you're good at."

An angry red rash rises up Beranabus's neck, but he doesn't respond. Instead he casts an eye over the demon-encrusted walls. "Agreed!" he says abruptly.

Lord Loss laughs and extends a hand towards us. "Eeny... meeny... miny..."

"Such games belittle you!" Beranabus barks. "Choose!"

"Very well." Lord Loss's hand points at me. Vomit creeps up my throat. I see the end coming, perishing in this horrible universe, far from home. I prepare myself to run, even though I know it's hopeless.

But then the hand moves on and settles on its real target — *Nadia!*

"Hah!" she shouts at Beranabus, all of her contempt for him contained in that one small sound.

Then she shoots across the room. Lord Loss grabs her out of the air. Wraps all eight arms around her. I see her eyes snap tight, her lips close, her face scrunch up with fear. There's a blinding flash of light. I cover my eyes until the glow fades. When I look again, Lord Loss is covered in blood, bits of flesh, and shards of bone and hair — all that's left of poor, pockmarked Nadia Moore.

THE CHALLENGE

→I can't believe it happened. I know it must have – the evidence is splattered all over Lord Loss and his arachnid throne – but still I can't take it in. Nadia can't be dead, not so suddenly, so bloodily. Surely, even this warped universe of horrors can't be that cruel.

While my brain's whirring, Cadaver shrieks and tosses Art at Lord Loss, then makes a break for freedom, racing to a wall which has slightly fewer demons on it, scuttling towards a window.

Lord Loss catches Art smoothly and cradles him to his chest, keeping him clear of the hole where the snakes are slithering over and under each other. Art laughs, undisturbed. Lord Loss whistles to the demons on the wall. They surge round the window, blocking it, driving Cadaver back.

The demon momentarily thinks about fighting then releases his grip and drops to the floor. In a crouch, he lets the hairs on his arms grow to their fullest length, glares at Lord Loss and waits for the demon master to make the next move.

Lord Loss chuckles at Art or Cadaver, I'm not sure which. Then he says something twisted — it must be a demon language. Cadaver falls to the floor, writhing and hissing. He rolls around, scratching at his throat and face. The demons on the walls laugh and screech at him.

Then, over the sounds of the demons comes a strangely mixed cry of fear and delight. Cadaver stops struggling and sits up. The cry comes again, and this time I realise it comes from Cadaver. He's been altered. He has a mouth.

"I have honoured my end of the bargain," Lord Loss says. Cadaver screams unintelligibly in response. "Such language," Lord Loss tuts. "I am glad most of my guests are not able to understand you or their ears would sizzle. I apologise, Beranabus. Such curses should not be uttered even in this universe."

"I've heard worse," Beranabus says. "Usually from demons I'm about to kill." Cadaver goes silent and shifts his attention to Beranabus, eyeing him suspiciously. Beranabus smiles icily. "Don't worry. If you answer my questions honestly – and that should be much easier now you have a mouth – I won't kill you. My advice is to come quietly. Fight if you wish, but without Lord Loss to protect you, we both know you can't win."

Cadaver bristles and looks at Lord Loss. He says something low and pleading. Lord Loss shakes his head. "No. I vowed to give you a mouth and voice, and promised to protect you until that time. I have acted in good faith. I owe you nothing more."

Cadaver sneers, then spits on the floor, putting his new mouth to good use. Facing Beranabus, he retracts his hairs and marches towards him with pride, offering himself to the magician, hateful but resigned. When Cadaver is by his side, Beranabus raises an eyebrow at Lord Loss.

"Go," the demon master says, waving at the demons round the door, who part at his command. He's smiling. His eyes flicker down at Art, then up at me. He knows this isn't over, that there's more miserable pleasure to be had.

Beranabus starts towards the door.

"Wait," I stop him. "What about Art?"

Shark, Sharmila and Dervish haven't moved. They're looking at Beranabus like I am, questioningly, aware of the promise he made.

"There's nothing we can do," Beranabus says without looking back.

"But you said—" I start to protest.

"That was before I knew Lord Loss ordered the theft," Beranabus snaps. "I thought if the child was alive we'd only have to pry him from Cadaver. But he's the demon master's plaything now. He's lost. Accept it."

"Toothy little Art," Lord Loss purrs, tossing him up into the air, grey teeth exposed, red eyes narrow slits. "Do you want to see what happens when *I* bite, Art?"

"Leave him alone!" I scream. I take a step towards Lord Loss. Stop. Glance back at Beranabus, wanting him to back me up. But he doesn't even turn his head.

As I waver, torn between wanting to save Art and knowing it means death to face Lord Loss by myself, Dervish steps up beside me. "I'm with you," he says quietly, causing my eyes to fill with grateful tears.

"It's madness," Shark says, taking up position on my other side, "but how could I leave a couple of kids behind?"

I smile at the ex-soldier, then look hopefully at Sharmila. She bites her lower lip and stares at Beranabus. He has turned and is studying us expressionlessly. Sharmila hesitates, starts to smile, then shakes her head. "I am sorry," she whispers. "It is hopeless. The first thing we learn as Disciples is not to throw our lives away. We have to choose our battles carefully and only fight those which we can win."

"Coward," Shark growls.

"No," Dervish says. "It's the sensible choice."

Lord Loss is beaming at us, loving this. "Such brave boys," he murmurs, tickling Art's chin, careful not to be bitten.

"I can't let you do this," Beranabus says. "I need you — especially Kernel."

"You were quick enough to offer our lives a minute ago," Shark reminds him.

"But now I have what we came for — Cadaver. I won't leave you to be needlessly slaughtered. I can force you to come with me."

"I only came for Art," I tell him. "There's no point trying to take me. Even if you could, it wouldn't do you any good.

I'd never open a window again, unless it was a window back to this place. Try me — see if I'm bluffing."

Beranabus sighs, then squints at Lord Loss. "Can we do a deal for the child?"

"Perhaps," Lord Loss replies smoothly. "But I'm not sure I want to. This is far more interesting. I'm dying to see if you will really abandon them, or if you and Miss Mukherji will also stay and fight."

"There's no chance of that happening," Beranabus says.

"You are certain?"

"Aye."

"Then the pair of you cannot be part of any deal," Lord Loss says, turning his attention to me. He strokes Art's head softly, cooing. Grins, eyes alive with evil. "How much do you love your brother, Cornelius?"

"Not enough to let you murder me for him," I reply, thinking about Nadia.

"You wouldn't give your life to save his?" Lord Loss asks, surprised.

"I'd risk it, but I won't throw it away."

"Interesting." Lord Loss purses his lips. After a few moments he calls, "Vein!"

A dog-shaped demon slithers down one of the walls. It looks like a black labrador with a crocodile's head and a woman's delicate hands instead of paws. She trots over to her master and waits by the foot of the spider-shaped throne.

"The Board," Lord Loss says, and the demon races out of the room.

Silence, waiting for the demon called Vein to return with whatever Lord Loss sent her for. I watch Art play in the demon master's arms, wishing I could be as ignorant of danger as my brother. While I'm thinking about that, my mind replays all that's been said. Frowning, I ask, "Why did you steal Art?"

"I didn't," Lord Loss says. "Cadaver took him."

"But you told him to. You hired him. Why? Was it to get at me? Did you know about my gift?"

"What gift?" Lord Loss asks.

"Careful," Beranabus warns. "Don't tell him anything about yourself."

"So it wasn't because you wanted me?" I press.

"No," Lord Loss says. "I remembered you from our previous encounter, but—"

"You've met before?" Beranabus barks, startled.

"Cornelius and I are old acquaintances," Lord Loss says. He smiles at me. "I guessed you would come after your brother, but I expected you to perish along the way. You held no interest for me then — although you certainly do now."

"It wasn't a trap?"

"Why go to all that effort to trap a boy I barely know?" Lord Loss laughs. "This gift of yours must be something very special if you think—"

"Kernel!" Beranabus barks.

I wave him quiet, letting him know I'm not stupid, that I'm taking care. "Why?" I ask again. "Why steal Art?"

Lord Loss smiles smugly. "That answer is tied in with the game I plan to let you play — assuming you're agreeable. Ah, here's Vein. We can begin."

I look around and see the crocodile-dog making for her master with a chess board grasped in her mouth. It's a few inches thick, made of glass or crystal. Beranabus's eyes widen when he sees the board. He starts towards Vein, as though to take the board from her, then stops and squints at Lord Loss. "Is that…?"

"Yes. The Board. The original."

"I thought it was lost for ever, deep beneath the earth."

"No. I rescued it."

"I can't play chess," I tell Lord Loss. "I know some of the rules, but not all of them."

"That's all right," Lord Loss says, floating down from his throne, taking the Board from Vein, wiping the surface clear of spit and slime. He looks at the black and white squares, smiling softly. "This is not a regular board. It is the very first chess board, given to humans by ancient beings who came to Earth from the stars. It was designed for greater things than chess, and since unlocking its secrets I no longer play upon it. The Board is better suited to other games. To battle."

"I don't understand," I frown.

Lord Loss sets the Board on the floor. "Size, like time, can be different here. In this universe, an object can be both immense and microscopic. The Board is tiny in form, but enormous within. It contains a variety of universes in which I can place the souls of you and your loyal friends. There is no physical exit. Only the truth can guide you out."

Lord Loss holds up three arms. "You came in search of a demon thief. Since there are three of you, I will give you three chances to find that thief inside the Board, to apprehend and name him. If you do, your brother will be returned to you and you can take him home, if that is your wish. Otherwise you will remain trapped in the Board for the remainder of your life — and that will be a long, slow, horrible life, Cornelius. One of unimaginable darkness and misery."

"No," Beranabus hisses. "You can't ask that of him. He's just a boy."

"Quiet!" Lord Loss bellows. "You had your chance to be a participant. Now be silent, like any other bystander."

I stare at the demon master, confused. "I don't get it. I know who the thief is. I already found him. Cadaver."

Lord Loss shrugs. "If you and your companions agree to this, I will separate your souls from your bodies – a painless process – and secure them within the Board. You must search for the demon thief there, just as you searched for him here. I'll give you three chances to find and name him. There is no time limit, but if you name the wrong thief on three occasions, your souls will remain captive in the Board. You'll live out the rest of your lives there, and those lives will last hundreds, maybe thousands, of years as you experience time."

He stops and waits for my answer.

I'm still not entirely sure about the rules. Why would I name another demon as the thief when I know it's Cadaver? Unless there will be others disguised as Cadaver and I have to separate the real thief from the fakes.

"What do you think?" I ask Dervish and Shark.

"Will we have to fight?" Shark asks Lord Loss.

"Oh, yes," Lord Loss says with relish.

"Can we die?" Dervish frowns. "I mean, if we don't have actual bodies…"

"Although I'll separate your souls from your bodies, you will retain your current forms when you enter the Board," Lord Loss explains. "If you are killed during the game, your makeshift bodies will dissolve and I will gain control of your souls."

Shark shrugs. "I don't quite get all that, but I'm still with you."

"Me too," Dervish says.

I smile at them, then face Lord Loss. "OK. We'll do it. But I want your word that—"

I get no further. Lord Loss barks a quick spell. Webs drop from the ceiling and ensnare us. We start to struggle, but then the webs go up in flames. I feel a stinging sensation. My body seems to melt away. I try to scream. A red veil passes over my eyes. Then the castle, demons and world around me blink out of existence.

AMAZEING

→Darkness. Silence. I'm crouched over, hands covering my head, trying to protect my face from the sizzling webs. Then I realise I'm not on fire. There's no pain. I relax my hands and sit up, brushing cobweb ash from my cheeks.

I can't see. Total blackness. I reach out with my hands but don't touch anything. "Hello?" I call, then wait for Shark or Dervish to respond.

No answer.

I get to my feet, stretch my hands out and start walking. I count steps inside my head. Ten. Fifteen. Twenty. Fifty. A hundred. On my hundred and thirtieth step, my left hand brushes something soft and sticky. I pause and explore with my fingers. It's a wall of webs. When I try ripping through the webs, they resist.

"Dervish!" I shout. "Shark!"

No answers. No echoes. Only silence.

→Walking, keeping one hand on the webby wall. I come to another wall after several minutes, blocking the way ahead. I turn right and follow the new wall. Only get twelve paces before striking another wall. So I'm either in a very long, narrow room or some sort of alley. Hand on the wall, I start back in the direction I came, trying hard not to panic.

After sixty-two paces there's a left turn. A long walk after that, the wall curving slightly. Then I come to the mouth of another room or alley. I head down it, left hand staying in touch with the wall. After twenty-two paces I come to another turning. I start to follow it around to the left then pause. I've had an idea.

Lowering my hand, I shuffle twelve paces across to the right and find the wall opposite. I continue straight ahead, right hand feeling the way. After thirty-six paces I come to a halt. Turn left. Walk ahead. Ten paces... twelve... twenty.

I stop, smiling ever so slightly. I know where I am now. In a maze.

A few seconds later, the smile fades — there's no telling how large this maze is or where the exit might be. Or even if there is an exit. I guess there's only one way to find out. Keeping a hand on the wall, I start ahead again, further into the pitch-black, demonic maze.

→I'm mapping the maze inside my head. I must have been here for hours. Trying to remember all the twists and turns I've taken, the paces between them. Focusing on numbers helps me not worry so much about the darkness, the silence, being all alone with no idea of where…

The darkness.

I come to a stunned stop, only now realising why I find the darkness so unsettling. It's *total* darkness — there aren't any patches of light! For the first time in my life I'm experiencing darkness as other people understand it. The lights I've grown up with – which I used to create windows between worlds in this universe – have disappeared.

A terrifying thought strikes like a missile — maybe I'm blind! Perhaps that's why the darkness is absolute. Maybe Lord Loss burnt my eyes out of their sockets and it's actually bright as day in here.

My heart thumps fast. My legs go weak. A life of blackness, lost in a maze, no friends to turn to for help… Maybe that's what Lord Loss meant when he said I had to find and name the demon thief. Perhaps that's why he was smirking. He knew that blind, I wouldn't have any way of identifying Cadaver. He's tricked me! Robbed me of my sight! Stranded me in this maze of eternal darkness!

I moan aloud, losing hope, the map of the maze disintegrating inside my head. I should have listened to Beranabus. What made me think I could strike a fair deal with a demon? I feel hysteria bubble up within me. Madness digs its claws into my brain, dragging its way to the surface.

Magic, a voice inside me whispers. *Use magic to create light. Then you'll find out if you're blind or not.*

"I don't know how to do that," I whimper.

This is a good time to learn, the voice says drily.

I nod slowly. The voice is right. No point freaking out when my eyes might be perfectly fine. I concentrate, drawing upon the magic. I'm not much good at fighting, but let's see how I fare in other areas.

I imagine a ball of light, small, not too bright, like the bulb in my bedroom at home. A simple ball of light — that can't be too much to ask for.

But it is. I can't generate one. Or else I've created light, but can't see it.

No, the voice says. *You'd know if you had done it. There is no light.*

"So I can't tell if I'm blind or not. Though I don't suppose it matters much. If this darkness holds, I might as well be blind."

The voice doesn't answer immediately. Then, as if speaking to a simpleton, it says, *Remember the chess board?*

"What about it?"

It had black squares and white squares. If those squares correspond to the worlds within the Board...

"...then half the maze is dark and half is bright!" I shout.

Exactly. So all you have to do is find your way to a white square. Then you'll see again.

"Unless I'm in a white square already and I'm blind," I quibble.

Just walk! the voice snaps.

*　　*　　*

→Stumbling through the maze. I've given up trying to keep track of my route. It's too large to map without a pen and paper (and light). I just have to keep walking and hope that I eventually find my way out by (blind) luck.

I think about the demon master's castle and how familiar it seemed. I wonder if I saw it that first time I crossed through a window into the universe of the Demonata. I guess there's a strong possibility that I did, especially given the fact that I saw Lord Loss beforehand.

I still can't remember anything about that trip. I try again to recall what happened when I vanished from my bedroom, where I went, if I came to Lord Loss's world. But it's a blank.

Thinking about that night reminds me of how lonely I was. Without the patches of light I feel lonely again, like before Art came along. I hated being an only child after Annabella died. I think I've risked so much for my brother not just because I love him, but because I'm afraid of being alone. He's the only true friend I've ever had.

For some reason, I find myself thinking about leaving our home in the city. Dad tucking me down in the back seat of the car, handing Art to me, covering us with a blanket, telling me to pretend we had to hide. Mum looking worried. "Take care of your brother, Kernel. Protect him."

Then my memory cuts to Art playing with the orange marbles in Sally's house. Holding them up, the marbles twinkling in front of his eyes. I had the sense that he'd been possessed by an evil spirit. That must have been a vision of what was to come. If Art remains with Lord Loss, and the demon master keeps him alive, will he raise him like one of his familiars? Give him evil powers? Bring him up to be monstrous... to kill?

The marbles are still in my pocket. I pull one out to have something to touch that isn't a webby wall. I roll it between my fingers, careful not to drop it. It helps calm me down. A pity I can't see — I could play a game with the marbles if I had some light.

As I think that, I feel magic seep through my fingers into the marble — and it starts to glow! A soft orange light. I gasp and clutch my fingers tight around it, scared my mind is playing tricks, not wanting to be disappointed.

Staring down at the space where I imagine my hand to be. Slowly, hesitantly, I allow my fingers to loosen — and light flashes through the cracks! With a burst of relief, I thrust my hand up and let more magic explode into the marble. It flares to life, causing my eyelids to snap shut. I pull back some of the power, then open my lids slowly, not looking directly at the marble.

I can see! I must have been in a black square of the maze all along, as my inner voice suggested. Not that sight is much of a bonus here. All I see are webby walls and a floor. Several feet above me hangs the ceiling, a mass of black webs, impossible to see through.

I smile weakly, gazing at the orange marble throwing off the light, feeling more grateful to it than I ever thought possible. I mean, how many people can say their lives have been enriched by a marble!

Then, because I can't stand here gazing at the marble all day like it's some godly artefact, I bring my hand down, hold it slightly ahead of me to light my path, and continue working my way through the seemingly endless maze.

→Not long after. Making my way down a narrow path much like any other, when I hear a sound somewhere ahead and to the left. I pause, listening carefully. Nothing for a few seconds. But then it comes again, a soft ripping noise, then giggling.

I advance cautiously, dimming the orange light. I think about letting it go out completely, but then not only wouldn't the person or creature around the corner not be able to see me — I wouldn't be able to see them.

I pause at the corner. Listen closely. More ripping sounds. An occasional giggle. I think about calling Dervish or Shark's name. Dismiss the idea — I never heard Dervish or Shark giggle like that.

I cup my fingers round the marble, directing the light upwards. Step forward, around the corner.

It takes my eyes a second to adjust. Then I make out a small shape sitting by the wall to my right, maybe fifteen feet ahead of me. A baby. Pulling at the webs, tearing handfuls out of the wall, eating them. "*Art!*" I shout, letting the light brighten and my fingers drop.

The baby whirls and of course it isn't my brother. I knew as soon as the shout left my lips that it wasn't. It's the same general size as Art, but green, with lice for hair, fire in its eye sockets and small mouths in the palms of its hands — the first demon I saw when I came to Lord Loss's world.

The hell-child spits out a mouthful of webs and hisses at me. I glare at him, hating him for not being Art, for raising my hopes and then dashing them. Not afraid. Despite the fact that I'm not much of a fighter, I'm confident that I can take this demon. He ran once already, which makes me suspect he's not the bravest of his kind.

"Come here," I mutter, stepping towards the hell-child, thinking he might know the way out. The demon shows his teeth and takes his own menacing step forward. But then he hesitates, glances around and darts away.

I grin viciously. I'm through being meek Kernel Fleck, unable to take care of himself. It's time for payback. With a wild whoop of abandonment, I give chase.

→I race through the maze, hot on the demon's heels, reckless with excitement. Taking corners without slowing, I bounce off the webby walls more than once, stick for a few seconds, then tear myself free. The hell-child squeals as he runs. That goads me on, makes me eager to catch up with him. The loneliness and uncertainty have vanished. The chase is everything.

I almost catch the demon a couple of times, when he hits walls and sticks to them. But he pulls free each time and escapes. His back and shoulders are covered in webs. I'm caked with them too, but I don't stop to wipe them away.

The demon disappears round a corner to my right. When I turn, I see we're at the start of an extra long path, and at the end of it... *light!* Too soon to tell if it's daylight or the light of a fire. Maybe it's the glow of some demon. But I race towards it regardless, focusing more on the light than the hell-child now, anxious to leave the darkness behind.

→Almost at the end of the path. I can tell now that the light is coming from overhead and it seems to be widespread. A dull, yellowish light.

The hell-child darts out of the maze and off to the left, out of sight. I'm at the exit a few seconds later. I pause before stepping out, in case it's a trap. I let the light of the marble fade, then replace it in my pocket. I flex my fingers – nervous now I've stopped – and cautiously nudge out.

A rocky landscape. There are lots of hills and mounds, and steam spurts out of the ground in many places. The stench of sulphur is thick in the air. In the near distance runs a river of bubbling lava. I know what it is because I've been to museums and seen videos of volcanic eruptions. I can't see the source of the river, but it can't be far away, since the lava's red-hot and liquid, flowing swiftly.

I spot the hell-child running towards the river. I'd like to explore, but I've got to maintain my focus and keep up the chase. Perhaps the demon knows where Dervish and Shark are, or Cadaver. Maybe he's Cadaver in disguise!

The hell-child reaches the river of lava and stops. Turns and faces me. Squealing louder than ever, head thrown back. I close in on him, ready for him to break left or right, trying to outguess him.

The demon stops squealing and glares at me. He looks like he plans to attack, but then, surprising me, he takes a step back — on to the river of lava. Steam rises from the demon's feet, and seconds later they burst into flames. But the hell-child only laughs and blows on them, extinguishing the fire. With a grin at me, he skips across the forty or fifty feet width of the river, jumping off at the other side, only the top of his head visible now.

I stop at the lava's edge. The heat is incredible. I feel my skin redden. I use magic to cool it, but even with the help of magic it's hard to bear. I stare at the lava uncertainly. If the hell-child was able to skip across, I probably can too. But what if I can't? What if my magic fails me? If I venture out on to the lava, and things take a turn for the worse, I'm finished. This body will rot away and Lord Loss will imprison my soul.

Trying to work up the courage to test the lava. I look left and right, in case there's some other way to cross, like a bridge or tunnel — but there's nothing. The river stretches as far as I can see in both directions.

As I'm looking around, my eyes flick up to see what the sky is like. But instead of a sky, I find myself gazing at the hideous face of Lord Loss! It's huge, filling my entire field of vision. He's laughing, though I can't hear him. I freeze, horrified by his immense red eyes, the pores and cracks in his skin, which look like moon craters and valleys when magnified to this extent. Then he pulls back and Beranabus replaces him. He's almost as ugly when seen from this perspective.

The magician is shouting at me, pointing with a finger the size of a battering ram. It takes me a few seconds to realise he's gesturing to a spot behind me — trying to warn me! I whirl defensively, but too late. I catch sight of a winged demon with a red, lumpy body, hurtling at me through the air. I duck instantly, but the demon has judged its flight perfectly. It hits me hard in the chest, driving me off my feet, backwards — into the river of molten lava.

MARBLEOUS

→Searing heat. I scream and thrash, splashing lava up into the air. I go under, immersed in the fiery liquid, feeling it fill my mouth, nose, ears, burning away the soft flesh of my lips and ear lobes, destroying my eyelids, setting to work on the jelly-like globes of my eyes.

I come up. Spit out lava. Scream again, tongue crackling, throat pinched tight, sizzling eyes wide with terror. I don't try using magic to protect myself. Panic has taken over. I'm helpless. Caught by the river. Lost.

I start to sink. My legs kick out automatically, like when I'm swimming, to keep my head up. Gasping for air. I feel my toes burning away, and the acid of the lava eats its way through the wall of my stomach. A few more seconds and it'll all be over. I'll just be scraps of flesh and bone smeared across the surface of the river — then nothing.

I hear a shout to my left, but I'm not able to look round. I'm going under. No lower legs left to kick with. Bones are showing through the flesh of my fingers. The skin of my throat is peeling back like burning paper.

Then hands snake around the remains of my chest and I'm hauled out of the lava. My lidless eyes focus blearily. It's a woman, her face contorted by my ruined eyes. She's yelling, but my ears are full of lava. I can't hear what she's saying.

The woman pulls what's left of me free of the river and races with me to the bank, dumping me on hard, cold land. Falls beside me, her feet and shins on fire. She slaps at the flames, then stops, stares, quenches them with magic.

I'm bubbling away to nothing beside her, covered with lava that's still eating through my flesh. When the woman has put out her own flames, she turns her attention to me. Shouts the words of a spell and waves a hand over me. The lava explodes off me in splatters, out of my nose, mouth and ears. I take an unbelievably welcome breath of air, then cry out my agony to the world.

"Kernel!" the woman yells. "You have to help me! The damage is too great — I can't repair it by myself."

I'm gasping like a dying fish, unable to respond. I never thought there could be so much pain this side of death. The woman casts another spell. A cool wave washes through me, numbing me to the worst of the torment. I draw back from the brink of pain-fuelled insanity. Lay my head down, moaning weakly instead of screaming madly.

"Use magic," the woman urges me. "Help yourself. Restore the flesh that's been burnt away. It'll hurt like hell, but you have to do it."

I want to say that I can't, I'm too weary and don't know the spells. But my incinerated vocal cords and lips won't let me form the words. Annoyed, I try to fix the damage, so I can tell the woman I'm finished. Magic flows to the areas which I've targeted and cells knit together in response to my command. As my lips return, bloody and stinging, but workable, I start to complain. Then I realise — the fact I *can* complain proves I *have* the power to heal myself. So instead of whinging, I set to work on the rest of my wrecked body.

It takes several minutes, and is every bit as painful as the woman predicted, but eventually, I'm almost whole again, scorched and blackened from the heat, pink new flesh glistening sorely in the yellow light, scarred around the places where I've had to create fresh flesh and bones, tender as... well, as somebody who'd been dunked in a river of lava! But I'm alive and mostly in one piece.

Smiling painfully, I lift my face to thank the woman who came to my rescue. I'm expecting Sharmila — I figure she couldn't stand by and watch me die, so she entered the Board to save me — but the face my new eyes fix on is much younger and paler than the Indian lady's. But just as familiar.

"*Nadia!*" I gasp.

She stares at me with an angry but wary expression. "You should have been prepared for an attack. You fell too easily. It would have served you right if I'd left you."

"But you're dead!" I cry.

She laughs. "Then you have a ghost to thank." She stands and looks into the distance. "Dervish is on his way. I was leading him to you when I sensed you fall into the lava." She starts to walk away.

"Wait! I don't understand! I saw you die. How can you be here?"

She hesitates and looks up. Following the direction of her gaze, I see that the sky is hazy now, cutting off my view of Lord Loss and Beranabus. "You must not tell him," Nadia says quietly.

"Tell who what?" I frown.

"Beranabus. That I'm alive." She faces me and now she wears a cool, flat look. "I had enough of it, Kernel. He treated me like scum, using me any way he wished. I had no freedom or say over my life. So I decided to trade allegiances and go where I'd be appreciated and rewarded."

"You mean...?" I can't bring myself to say it.

"I joined Lord Loss," she whispers. "I spoke to him secretly when we arrived at his castle. Told him of my gift. Promised to serve him if he'd allow me a few simple pleasures and some time to myself."

"But he's a demon!" I shout. "They kill humans!"

"Yes," she answers smoothly.

I gawp at her, unable to believe it. She shifts uneasily and looks away. "Beranabus can't see us now. He'll never know I'm alive. Unless you tell him."

"But Lord Loss is our enemy. You—"

"I saved your life!" she snaps. "I didn't have to. I could have left you to sink."

"Why did you save me?" I ask softly.

"Because I like you." She laughs and there are tears in her eyes. "I like all of you — except Beranabus. I hate him, with good reason. But I don't wish harm to anyone else. I came here to hide. Lord Loss separated my soul before destroying my body — or most of it. He kept my brain and heart whole. He can put my flesh and bones back together around them later, and restore my soul from here. When I felt you and the others enter the Board, I asked Lord Loss if I could help you. He said I could, but only once. So this is it. You're on your own now."

"Nadia... you mustn't do this. Lord Loss is evil. If you stay with him, he might ask you to do evil things."

"I'm certain he will." She shrugs. "But I no longer care. I've been apart from humans so long, I don't feel like I have anything in common with them. This might be the last decent act I ever perform. But I'm fine with that. If I'm to become like the Demonata... like my new master..." She draws herself up straight, blinking the tears away, eyes flashing. "So be it."

"Nadia..." I try again, but she stops me.

"I saved your life, Kernel. In return, I'd like you to keep my secret and tell no one I'm alive. I can't make you promise, but I'll be disappointed if you betray me."

"I won't tell," I mutter.

"Thank you." She smiles awkwardly, but it quickly fades. "One last warning. If you escape this Board and our paths cross in the future, we'll be on different sides. Don't expect me to ever help you again."

With that, she turns, raises her face to the sky, extends her arms, then turns into a beautiful, swan-like demon. As I watch, she gracefully rises and glides away, picking up speed, soaring higher and higher, until she's only a speck against the skyline... then gone.

→Dervish arrives some time later. I'm lying in the same spot, still in agony, using magic to make little changes and tweaks. As Dervish fusses over me, I tell him about the attack and my fall, but claim I pulled myself out and patched my body together unassisted. I don't mention Nadia.

"Can you stand?" Dervish asks, fanning his face, sweating from the heat of the river.

"I don't think so," I croak.

"How about levitate?"

I manage a chuckle. "I'm not Beranabus. I can't fly."

"Then I'm going to pick you up," he says. "We need to get away from here. I'll be as gentle as possible. Ready?"

I nod, gritting my teeth so I don't cry out too loudly when he touches me. As carefully as he can, Dervish sneaks one arm under my neck, the other beneath my knees, and lifts. It's not as bad as I thought, but I can't stop myself from gasping and shutting my newly grown eyelids against the pain.

"Sorry," Dervish says, then hobbles away from the lava, carrying me like a baby.

→Resting behind a hill, sheltered from the heat of the river. I'm still working on my body, using magic to undo the damage and smooth over the cracks. Make sure all my bones are solid. Regrow fingernails and fingerprints. Separate my toes. Try to get my ears the right shape. Let warm energy circulate through my legs, strengthening them, knowing I'll have to get up soon and walk.

No more faces in the sky. Just a ceiling of yellow light. I asked Dervish about them, but he didn't see Lord Loss or Beranabus. He'd been wandering like me, but in this zone of light, not darkness. Then he spotted a white, winged demon. Since it seemed to be the only living creature, he followed it until it vanished. Having no better plan, he kept going in the same direction — and found me.

"Where do you think Shark is?" I ask.

Dervish shrugs. "He could be anywhere. I've no idea how large this place is." I tell him my idea, that it's laid out like a chess board, thirty-two dark areas, thirty-two light zones. Dervish hadn't thought of that. "I think you're right," he says. "But we've no way of working out the size of each square."

"Did you find any water?" I ask. "I'm thirsty."

"Don't think about it," he advises. "You can keep thirst and hunger at bay, like sleep. Your body will do almost anything you tell it here."

He strokes his spikes of hair, stiff and upright again, a few inches longer than before. He's putting on a brave front, but I can see he's terrified. He's not much older or more experienced than me. He's never been in a situation like this. He's acting grown-up, but I bet – like me – he'd give anything to have somebody to turn to for help.

"We need a plan," I say, wanting to make things a bit easier for Dervish. "We can't just stagger around, waiting to be attacked. We should have a purpose."

"Getting the hell out of here would be a good start," Dervish mutters.

"Yes, but Lord Loss said we could only get out if I found and named the demon thief. First, I think we should find Shark. Then we can try to figure out a way to unearth Cadaver."

Dervish nods. "That sounds good. But how will we look for Shark? Just pick a direction at random?"

"I suppose…"

"But what if we're in a square at one end of the Board and he's in a square at the opposite end?"

"Then it'll be a long walk."

Dervish laughs.

"What else can we do?" I ask.

Dervish frowns. "Maybe one of the demons could lead us to him — the hell-child or the winged monster." He walks around to the other side of the hill to look for them. Returns a minute later, shaking his head.

"There will be others," I say. "Lord Loss won't want to watch us walk around in circles for too long. That would be boring. I bet he'll send lots of demons to attack us."

"Great." Dervish doesn't sound too optimistic.

"I could use the patches of light to find Shark, except there aren't any here. The Board isn't like the outside universes. The rules are different."

Dervish chuckles. "From one universe of insanity to another."

"Maybe I could…" I stop and dig the marbles out of my pocket, remembering how I used one to create light in the maze of darkness.

"What are those?" Dervish asks.

"Marbles. My brother was playing with them before he was kidnapped."

"Oh. I was hoping they were some sort of magical globes."

"Maybe they are… or can be." I tell him about the maze, how I tried to create light but couldn't, until I got one of the marbles out.

"But we don't need light here," Dervish says.

"Thanks for pointing out the obvious," I snap. "What I meant was, if I could use a marble as a torch, maybe I could use it as some other instrument. Like a compass or a tracking device?"

Dervish looks sceptical but says, "Well, go on, give it a try."

I study the orange marbles and again find myself thinking of that night in Sally's house, Art holding them up over his eyes. Shutting the image out, I focus on thoughts of Shark, asking the marbles to lead me to him. Nothing happens immediately, but then Dervish gasps and leans in closer. The orange swirls at the heart of the marbles have turned mist-like, and through the mist we can see Shark, battling demons, his hands wet with blood.

"Where is he?" Dervish cries.

"I don't know." I try to bring the land around Shark into clearer focus but can't. Abandoning that tactic, I let the pictures of him fade and ask the marbles to guide us to him. They quiver in the palm of my hand, then leap into the air like jumping beans. I cringe away from them. Dervish does too. But when they just hang there, we recover and grin at each other. I get to my feet, Dervish helping me. Pain flares afresh, but I use magic to fight it. Then I focus on the marbles, still hanging in the air above us.

"Shark," I say quietly, directing my magic towards the marbles. They dart off ahead of me at a furious speed, twin bolts of orange lightning. "Wait!" I shout. They come to a halt, hovering in the air like bees. I glance at Dervish and he claps slowly.

I stumble forward, feet still blistered from the lava, Dervish supporting me. As we come up to the marbles, I again ask them to lead us to Shark. "But slowly," I add. "Don't get too far ahead of us." The marbles bob in the air, as though nodding, then float smoothly over the volcanic landscape, leading us in search of our demon-tormented friend.

KERNEL IN THE
SKY WITH DEMONS

→We march slowly but steadily, saying little, following the marbles. I try to keep track of time and distance, but it's impossible. Sometimes, I wish a demon would attack, just to break the monotony, but we see none of Lord Loss's familiars. We can't even sleep — our bodies get weary, but we can't shut off our brains.

Eventually, we come to a point where two enormous black panels meet at a ninety degree angle and run up to the roof of yellowish sky. The panels are several feet wide and half a foot thick. They stand alone in the rocky surroundings, eerily out of place.

"Have you seen the film *2001: A Space Odyssey?*" Dervish asks after a minute of silence.

"No. Why?"

"This reminds me of it." He walks round the black pillars, squinting at them, then says in a curiously flat voice, "Good morning, Dave."

"Who's Dave?"

Dervish laughs. "Doesn't matter." He looks at me, eyebrow cocked. "What do you think they are?"

"A place where four squares of the Board meet."

"Me too. But why just these weird slivers of black? I would have expected walls stretching the entire length of the boundaries."

"Why don't we step through one and see? I mean, we'll have to anyway, since the marbles were heading that way." The marbles stopped when we did, and now hang a few inches short of the black panel on our left.

"Let's try the right panel first," Dervish suggests. "Just for the hell of it."

"OK." I pick the marbles out of the air and put them in my pocket.

Dervish tests the panel, sticking a hand through to make sure we can pass. "It's OK," he says. "We—"

Suddenly, with a startled grunt, he disappears, hauled through the panel by something on the other side. I scream his name. When there's no response, I dart into the darkness after him.

→It's not pitch-black like the maze, but very dark. I get glimpses of a demon wrapping itself round Dervish. Tentacles covered in long, glistening blades, slicing away at Dervish, cutting him open, blood flying in every direction.

I jam my hand into my trouser pocket. Yank out both marbles. Scream a word of magic at them, the word coming from somewhere deep inside me. Light flares, sharp and fierce in its orange brightness. I yell another word of magic as the light bursts forth, directing all the rays towards the demon.

The demon shrieks with pain from the explosion of light. It has dozens of eyes, a necessity in this dark kingdom, but a handicap when strong light's trained on it. With another agonised cry, it releases Dervish and hurls itself away, sheltering its eyes with its tentacles.

I grab Dervish and throw him back through the panel, which is white on this side. Then I reverse out after him, at the last possible second commanding the marbles to follow, stepping through at the same time as they slip out of the dark zone, so I don't lose track of them.

Dervish is on the volcanic floor, healing his wounds with magic, angry for being caught out so easily. "Thanks," he mutters.

"Don't worry about it." I squat next to him. "Can I help?"

"No. I'll be fine once I patch myself up."

"A few of your spikes were cut off," I tell him, tapping his head.

"Maybe I'd be better off bald like you," he laughs, then makes the hair grow back to its proper length.

When he's healed himself, he stands, checks for any cuts he might have missed, then warily faces the other black panel. "There could be a similar monster through there. Or worse."

I say nothing. I want to volunteer to go ahead of him, to test the waters, but I'm afraid. Sheepishly hoping Dervish will take the lead.

Dervish breathes out through his nose, then glances at me. "Ready to save my bacon again?"

"If I have to," I chuckle then give the order for the marbles to lead us to Shark. They float through the panel into blackness. We follow.

→Space. Freezing emptiness. Not even air. A moment of complete dizziness and suffocating panic. Then instinct makes me surround myself with a force field of warmth and air. Dervish has done the same and is floating beside me, staring around with happy wonder. His mouth moves, but I can't hear what he's saying. I point to my ears and shake my head. He tries again, then makes a tube of air grow from his force field to mine. When it touches, he speaks and this time I hear him. "I always wanted to be a spaceman, like Flash Gordon. It was my dream."

"Me too," I smile. "Except I wanted to be a real astronaut, like Neil Armstrong or Buzz Aldrin. Walk on the moon."

"It's bizarre, isn't it?"

"Yeah. Like when we were on top of the cloud, but stranger."

Dervish does a slow somersault. It looks graceful at first, but he can't stop and keeps tumbling over and over. He yells for help, but I'm laughing too much at the freewheeling punk. Finally, he finds his balance, rights himself and glares at me. "Thanks for the help!"

"Do it again," I coo. "Whirl for me, Dervish, whirl!"

"I'll whirl my foot up your ass," he grumbles, then looks for the marbles. "Let's go find Shark."

"OK. But if you want to try your hand at gymnastics again, I'll be more than happy to—"

"Keep it up," he growls. "Keep it up!"

Laughing, I give the marbles their freedom and we drift forward again, leaving behind a pair of small white panels, glowing softly in the vacuum of sterile space.

→I was wrong about this space being sterile. Though there don't seem to be any planets, the marbles eventually lead us towards a demon of unbelievable size. It's one of the vast sky demons. From the ground they looked huge, but up here it goes beyond words like massive and immense. This one must be hundreds of miles long, fifty or sixty high, a comet-sized, slug-like demon, drifting through the void of space in search of... what? Demons to kill and devour? Foes to fight? A world to settle on?

Dervish and I pause when the marbles home in on the demon. We look at each other bleakly. "If that thing spots us..." Dervish whispers.

"We're too small," I whisper back, even though there's no need — sound can't carry in space, so we should be able to speak as loudly as we like. "It won't bother with a couple of ants like us."

"Unless it enjoys squashing ants."

We want to pull back, detour around it or wait for it to pass. But the marbles keep tugging after the demon, urging us to follow. Since we've no other option, we glide after them as they lead us ever closer to the terrifying behemoth.

→We come up underneath the monster's bulging stomach, which looks more like rock than flesh. The marbles pause next to the stomach wall. I get the sense they want to penetrate the demon's crusty shell. But then they take a turn and lead us forward, towards the creature's head.

Half an hour later, we float up from beneath the demon's gigantic lower jaw. I'm worried that, this close, the monster can't help but see us. But there's no evidence of any eyes. Either they're set much higher up its face or it's blind.

But there's definitely a mouth, running like a ridged valley from one side of the head to the other. Lips parted, teeth the size of large houses set in the rocky gums at irregular intervals. A tongue crawling with scores of smaller, parasitical demons, feeding on the remains of whatever this monster eats.

And amidst those demons, fighting for his life — *Shark*.

The warrior is in poor shape. These demons are weak compared with some of the others we've fought, small in size and power. But there are hundreds of them and they keep coming at him, fresh scavengers replacing the dead almost as soon as they've fallen. They're like tiny piranha bringing down a mighty ox.

"Shark!" Dervish bellows, but of course he can't hear. Dervish looks sideways at me, tilting his head instead of asking the question outright.

"I'm ready if you are," I tell him, though my stomach's tight with nerves.

"If the giant closes its mouth, I don't know if we could get out. Maybe only one of us should—"

"Don't tempt me," I stop him. "You and Shark risked everything to help me. It's only fair I do the same in return. So don't give me the option of cutting out on you now. I'm afraid I might take it."

Dervish grins. "Then let's go for a dip in the mouth of Moby Dick!"

→Cavernous. No smells or sounds. Just the spectacle of legions of vicious demons wriggling over and around one another to take turns attacking the lonely but resilient Shark. They spot us when we enter. Dozens peel away from the main assault and hurl themselves at us. Small, furry, dark demons, like tumbleweed with claws and fangs. We swat them aside without slowing. We've come too far and seen too much to be scared by these hangers-on.

Shark glances up as we close in on him. His eyes are distant and I see that he thinks we're another couple of demons. He aims a fist at me, but I stop out of range. Dervish dips lower, trying to direct a tube of air at Shark so they can communicate. But Shark must think it's a tendril or tongue. He ducks, throws demons at Dervish, edges away from him, further back the mouth. I flash on an image of what would happen if the monster swallows now. Quickly try to purge my mind of it.

I slip behind Shark and send out a tube of my own, all the time battling the demons. Shark spots the tube, dodges it, then leaps, hands outstretched, intent on throttling me.

Dervish flies forward and collides with Shark. They crash into me and our limbs get entangled. Now that we're touching, sharing our force fields, we can hear Shark. He's screaming madly, vile curses, words that make no sense, desperation and isolation thick in his throat.

"Shark!" Dervish roars. "It's us! Dervish and Kernel! We've come to rescue you. Stop fighting. We can get you out of here."

Shark screams in response, raises a large tattooed fist to pound Dervish flat, then pauses, faint lines of realisation rippling across his face.

"It's really us, Shark," I tell him. "This isn't a trick. We came for you."

"Impossible," he croaks. "How could you get here? You're illusions. Lord Loss sent you to torment me with hope."

"Don't be a dope," Dervish snaps. "Could any illusion look this good?"

Shark blinks — then grins. "*How?*" he whispers. "How did you find me?"

"We used magic."

"But it's empty space out there."

"So?"

"You mean... all this time... I could have left? I wasn't trapped? I didn't have to spend months... years... whatever... fighting these horrible furballs?"

"Nope," Dervish says lightly.

Shark's expression darkens. He grabs one of the demons and rips it to pieces, then uses its fur to wipe blood from his face. When he tosses the rag away, his features are composed. He sniffs as if what's happened is no big deal. "So much for the tour," he says casually. "Let's go find a bar."

Laughing, Dervish pats Shark on the back, points him towards the open mouth and guides him out of the maw of the monster, away from the gnashing teeth of the furious furry creatures, into the empty depths of darkest, coldest space.

→Floating, the monster having drifted on, we tell Shark about our adventures and theory that we're in a chess board-shaped universe of thirty-two different zones. He listens quietly, distracted, looking around twitchily. Sighs when we finish, then says softly, "Thanks for coming."

"We need you," Dervish says.

"For what?" Shark snorts. "You were doing fine without me. You figured this place out and dealt with it. All I did was stay where I had something solid underfoot. I thought that was going to be the rest of my life, that mouth and those demons. Part of me wanted to surrender and let them…"

He shivers, looking very different from the Shark I first met. The fight has drained him of much of his confidence and strength. I want to say something to make him feel better, but Dervish speaks before I can put my words together.

"I think Lord Loss knows you're the strongest of us. He wanted to break you, wear you down and kill you off, so you couldn't help Kernel. That's why he stuck you in the bleakest spot he could find and did all he could to destroy you. But he failed. You're alive. You survived where any other would have perished. So forget the self-pity. You had it tough, you dealt with it — now move on, soldier."

Shark laughs. "Nice speech."

"But true," Dervish adds.

"Maybe." Shark's laugh turns to a chuckle. "I guess I'm not cut out to suffer nobly, am I?"

"No. You've had your few minutes of moping — now put them behind you and let's work on getting out of this place and finding that bar you mentioned."

Shark grunts and faces me, recovering in the blink of an eye. I wish I had skin as thick as his, that I could go from the depths of despair to normality in the space of a few heartbeats. "Are those marbles still working?" he asks.

"I guess."

"Think you can use them to find this thief of yours?"

"Possibly."

"Then set the hounds loose, boy — it's time to kick demonic ass!"

THIEVES

→Nothing happens when I ask the marbles to lead me to the demon thief. So I ask them to find Cadaver instead, and they immediately set off, guiding us through the vastness of space. We'd be lost without the marbles. Impossible to tell up from down in this void. We couldn't even find our way back to the panels we came through. I wonder if Lord Loss knew about the marbles when he sent us here. Perhaps we have an advantage he didn't count on.

→After what feels like less than a day we come to a pair of white panels. The marbles hesitate, then split, one going left, one right. I stop them before they slip through. Glance at Dervish and Shark for their opinions.

"Looks like it doesn't matter which way we go," Dervish says.

"But Cadaver can't be in two zones at once, can he?" Shark frowns.

"Maybe he's straddling them," Dervish suggests. "A foot in each world."

"Or maybe the marbles are trying to split us up," Shark says suspiciously. "We don't know where their power comes from. This might be the work of Lord Loss — he separates us, throws us together, then splits us up again."

"I doubt it," Dervish says. "Anyway, if that's the case, it's easy to outfox him — we just don't part. We go through one panel together. Kernel, which do you prefer?"

I shrug. "I've no idea."

"Then let's go left," Dervish decides. When neither of us objects, he moves to a spot just behind me, Shark slides up in front, and in a close line we follow the marbles through the panel, into a new zone of fresh horrors.

→Guts everywhere. Every sort of inner organ imaginable. Stacked in piles, splattered around in pieces, some draping off trees of bone. A foul stench. The ground beneath our feet slippery with blood, mucus and all sorts of slime. I choke from the stench, vomit spewing out of my mouth. Dervish and Shark are the same. All three of us on our knees, vomiting, clutching our noses shut, gasping for air.

Demons are slithering through the mass of guts, ripping them apart, bathing in the blood and goo, feeding greedily. Most are worm-like, some as short as caterpillars, others several feet long. They're blind. They carry on shredding and guzzling, ignorant of our presence. One slides over the back of my legs, sniffs at me, decides there are richer pickings elsewhere and moves on.

"Magic!" Dervish gasps, eyes red and watery. "Create a… field… like in… the last place!"

It's hard to focus. The magic doesn't come easily here. The stench is foul, but it isn't fatal, so my body doesn't automatically generate a magical force field. After a minute or two of fumbling, I construct a weak field of air round my face. It's not as strong as the field I created in space, and some of the smell seeps through, but it blocks out the worst and allows me to breathe normally.

Shark finds it more difficult than Dervish or me. His magic isn't designed for subtle spells. With Dervish's help, he manages to create half a field around the front of his face, but it soon flickers out of existence. In the end he curses, rips a sleeve off his shirt and wraps it round his mouth and nose. For Shark, that's as good as it's going to get.

"Let's backtrack," Dervish says, nodding at the black panels behind us. "Try the other panel. It can't be any worse than—"

"Wait," I stop him. The marbles have darted forward and are hovering above a pile of pink and brown intestines. The guts heave upwards regularly, then subside, as though the pile is breathing. There must be a demon underneath, feasting on the guts, burrowing through them like a rat.

I advance slowly, digging my toes into the soft ground so I don't slip, only now realising that it isn't really ground, simply a floor of guts. Maybe we're inside the stomach of a huge demon like the sky monster. If so, I hate to think of where we might have to pass through to get out!

I'm almost level with the base of the pile when the guts on top are thrust off. A demon sticks its head out of the mess and happily shakes it hard from side to side. A green head, a cross between a human's and a dog's, with long draping ears and wide, white eyes.

"Cadaver!" I roar, startling the demon. When his eyes focus on me, he snarls, claws himself out of the pile of guts and scrabbles away across the floor of intestines.

"After him!" Shark yells, words muffled by his mask. He bounds over the pile of guts, slips and slides into a filthy pool of green and brown liquid. Comes up vomiting again, tearing his mask loose, wheezing for air.

Dervish darts to Shark's aid while I jog after Cadaver, not too fast, knowing it's better to go slow and keep my balance than speed up and slip as Shark did.

With his long legs and hairy feet – the hairs acting as grips – Cadaver soon pulls away from me, weaving around mounds of guts and leaping over murky, bubbling pools of blood and waste. I don't worry about losing track of him — the marbles are hot on his trail, obeying my orders, dogging the demon.

Cadaver treads on one of the longer worm-like monsters. It squeals and writhes beneath him, knocking him over. He screeches with his newly created mouth, hairs on his arms lengthening. Lashes out at the worm, slicing open a long gash down its side. Coiled layers of guts ooze out, adding to the ghoulish stew around it. The worm thrashes wildly, knocks Cadaver down again, pins him beneath its fleshy carcass. Cadaver slashes at the worm with his hairy arms and chews his way through strands of gut which have wrapped round his snout. He soon wriggles free — but by then I've caught up with him.

I grab Cadaver's ears and slam him down on top of the dying worm demon. I'm roaring triumphantly. Cadaver yowls and tries slapping me away. The hairs of one hand graze the side of my face, slicing my right cheek open. But the blood only drives me on with more passion. I grab his throat and throttle him, forgetting what Lord Loss said about naming the thief, intent only on killing this vile beast.

The hairs of Cadaver's hands snake around my neck and tighten, forming a lasso. We're strangling each other, face to face, snarling. The first to weaken will be the first to die.

My fingers begin to relax. I glare at them, willing them to close again, to finish the job they started. But they don't obey. I'm losing — perhaps I've already lost. Cadaver is grinning. The hairs tighten another notch, biting into the flesh of my throat, cutting off the last of my air supply. I feel my mouth gasping, eyes bulging, fingers scrabbling at the hairs instead of Cadaver's throat, trying to undo them.

Then a dripping, stinking Shark is beside me. A tattooed fist smashes Cadaver between the eyes. The demon grunts and the hairs loosen. Shark hits him again. The hairs slip away. I topple. Dervish catches me and props me up while Shark pummels Cadaver, beating all the fight out of the demon.

I breathe again, painfully, oxygen trickling through to my lungs. It feels like my throat has been crushed to splinters. Dervish places my hands on my wounded flesh and says, "Magic." I repair the damage. It doesn't take long. I'm getting used to fixing up my body.

When my throat's working normally, I check on Shark and Cadaver. The ex-soldier is still hitting the demon, but with less force, just to keep him in place. Shark catches my eye and winks. "You can take him off my hands or leave him to me for a few hours. I don't mind either way."

"It's OK," I tell him. "You've done enough. Thanks."

Shark steps away and I take his place. Cadaver glowers at me, his face bruised and bloody. I hear Shark complaining about the stench and how he doubts he'll ever be able to wash himself clean. I tune him out and focus. Recall Lord Loss's words. Touch Cadaver's forehead. Start to call him the demon thief.

Then stop.

Is this really the one who stole Art? Maybe it's another demon in disguise and Lord Loss is trying to trick me. I look for the marbles and find them floating a few feet above us. "Locate Cadaver," I mutter and they immediately strike at the demon beneath me, causing him to yelp and turn his head aside. I grab the marbles, stick them in my pocket, then –

with one hand still on Cadaver's forehead — shout, "This is the demon thief!"

Nothing happens. I was expecting a flash of lightning, a peal of thunder or an earthquake, something suitably dramatic. But there's no difference. I start to shout it again, in case I wasn't heard the first time. But somebody claps before I get the words out. I whirl and spot Lord Loss, floating in the air thirty feet above us, smiling sadly, applauding sarcastically.

"Such courage and imagination, Cornelius," the demon master murmurs. "The marbles were an excellent idea. They're only ordinary marbles, but you made them a catalyst for your magic, channelled your power through them. That spoilt my fun slightly — brought us to this juncture sooner than I anticipated — but I cannot bear a grudge. You are a true Disciple and master of magic."

He stops clapping and sighs. "But you miscalled the name of the thief. Cadaver is not the guilty party. One chance gone — you have two more."

"No!" I scream as Cadaver shuffles backwards, sneering at me. "He stole Art! It's him, not a demon in disguise! It's Cadaver!"

"Yes," Lord Loss agrees pleasantly. "It *is* Cadaver. But he is not the true demon thief."

"But... he must be... he..."

Inspiration strikes. Lord Loss said I had to find the *true* thief. Cadaver was a hired stooge. A puppet in the hands of his employer. He carried out the actual theft of Art, but he wasn't the brains behind it. The real thief must be the one who planned it, gave the order and paid the bounty.

I crouch, directing magic into my legs. Fix on Lord Loss. Adjust my aim. Then launch myself at him, flying through the air, leaping like a frog or cricket, covering the thirty feet in the flash of an eyelid.

Lord Loss is taken by surprise. He brings his eight hands together to ward me off, but too late. I have hold of him before he can repel me. Digging my fingers into his lumpy flesh – dough-like in feel as well as appearance – I scream at him, sure I'm right this time. "*You're* the true thief!"

Lord Loss throws me down. I hit a bulging sac of intestines. It explodes, showering me with blood, an acidy liquid and fragments of guts. I laugh carelessly, wallowing in the mess as though taking a bath, jeering at Lord Loss, smug at having beaten him at his own game. Dervish and Shark are staring at me uncertainly. They don't have my insight. They're not sure I'm right. But I am. As sure as I've ever been of anything. All that's left now is for Lord Loss to…

"Very clever, Cornelius," he says, cutting short my celebration. "But not clever enough, my poor young friend. I am *not* the true thief.

"Two chances gone — one remains."

His smile is chilling.

THE TRUE THIEF

→"You're lying!" I scream.

Lord Loss shakes his head slowly. "I do not lie."

"You have to be the thief! You gave the order for Art to be stolen! If Cadaver isn't the thief, it can only be you!"

"But it isn't," he says calmly. "Doubt my word if you wish, but Beranabus knows it is sacred. He is watching this now. If I lied to you, he would have cause to seek revenge. And while I do not fear Beranabus, I would rather not provoke him, especially when there is no need.

"Search again, Cornelius Fleck. Look for the *real* demon thief. You will find him if your heart is true and your eyes are clear. Then you will understand. And be set free." He raises a hand warningly. "But you have only once chance left. If you make a third wrong call, your souls are mine, as we agreed."

I feel angry tears in my eyes. Blink them away. I'm still not sure if he's telling the truth, but I've no choice other than to believe him. I have to focus. Think. If it's not Cadaver or Lord Loss, then *who*? Trying to make sense of it. Crazy thoughts flickering through my head —

→Maybe Beranabus struck a bargain with Lord Loss to steal Art. He might have sensed my power and wanted to draw me into this universe.

→Mrs Egin? The witch opened the passageway for Cadaver. Perhaps she was the true thief. But she's dead. Unless, like Nadia, her soul has been preserved here.

→Mum and Dad? Maybe they got into trouble or craved power, sold Art to Lord Loss, arranged for him to be kidnapped when they were away.

Madness. But the way my mind is whirring, I can almost believe it. I could believe the worst of just about anyone right now. Dervish, Shark, Sharmila — they're all suspects. Maybe the thief doesn't have to be a demon. It might be one of my closest allies.

Dervish steps up beside me and speaks in my right ear. "Don't like to rush you, Kernel, but we have company."

I look around and spy the demons from Lord Loss's castle. He's brought them into the Board with him. They're creeping up on us, sliding over and around the chains and hills of guts. I spot the crocodile-headed demon — Vein — off to my left, flanked by the fire-eyed hell-child. Advancing steadily along with the others.

My gaze passes on, then stops and returns to the hellish baby. I keep seeing him since I came to Lord Loss's kingdom. First when we arrived, then in the castle, the maze and volcanic zone, now here. Why does this demon cross my path more than any other? He's a fearsome little beast, with his fiery eyes, lice-ridden head and mouths in the palms of his hands. But no more frightening or vicious than a hundred of his kin. What draws me to him time and time again?

"We need to move," Shark says, nudging me hard in the ribs. "We can get out if we act fast, but in another minute they'll have blocked the path to the panels and we'll have to fight."

"It's one of them," I mutter, glancing at the hordes of demons, then at the hell-child again. "The thief's here. I'm certain."

*But you were **certain** it was Lord Loss*, the voice inside my head says, the first time for ages that it's spoken.

"It has to be one of them!" I cry.

Unless it's Beranabus, or Dervish, or your father, the voice says, and I don't know whether it's mocking my earlier hysteria or hinting I was on the right track.

"Kernel!" Dervish hisses. "We have to decide *now*!"

"Do not rush him," Lord Loss murmurs. "It is a hard, momentous decision. You should give it more thought, Cornelius. Escape. Rest. Ponder. You have more time than you could possibly imagine. Wait a hundred years, then try again. You don't want to act on a hunch, do you? Risk all on a blind gamble?"

"He's right!" Shark shouts, grabbing my arm and turning me in the direction of the panels. "Survival first — strategy second. Let's get the hell out while we—"

I pull free of Shark. "No! We'll never be free if we don't find him now! It's the hell-child! It must be! I keep seeing him!"

"You can't know that, Kernel," Dervish says. "Not for sure. Why him?"

"I don't know! I just..."

Cursing, I race after the hellish child, ignoring the threat of the demons and the possibility of escape. I'm gambling, a bigger gamble than any I've ever taken, but I have to. This is the moment when everything will be decided. That's why Lord Loss is here. He wants to see me fail, be here in person to gloat. But I can't worry about failing. I have to believe this is my chance, my time. And pray to all the gods that I don't waste it.

The hell-child sees that I've set my sights on him. He squeals with surprise, turns and flees. Vein snarls and sets herself between us, blocking my path to the demonic baby. Other demons pile in around her, increasing my belief that the hell-child is the thief.

"Shark!" I roar. "Dervish! Help me get through!"

They answer my call without question, placing their faith and future in my hands. They drive ahead, savaging the demons, Shark pounding them with his fists, Dervish scattering them with bolts of magic. I try not to dwell on the trust these men have shown in me, the awful fate which awaits them if I let them down.

A demon made entirely of bones throws itself at my legs. I kick out at it, smash its jaw, leap over the pieces of skeleton as they clatter to the ground. I've passed Dervish. Shark is wrestling with demons just ahead of me, to my right. "Leg-up!" I shout and Shark crouches, cups his hands together, holds them out for me to step into. Then hurls me up, forward and over the heads of the demons in front of us.

I hit the floor running. Almost skid on the guts and go flying into a pool of gore, but flail with my arms and keep my balance. The hell-child is directly ahead of me, looking back, snarling with a mix of hate and fear. My speed propels me past him. I snatch wildly as I race past, unable to slow. Grab one of the demon's bony arms. Haul him forward with me, the hell-child shrieking like a real baby.

My feet go and this time I don't try to stay upright, concentrating instead on holding on to the demon. I tumble over and slide several feet, smack up against a towering pile of organs. The guts shake then topple, smothering me and the hell-child. My field of air shatters. The foul stench causes me to vomit again, but I don't let go of the wriggling, furious demon.

A brief pause to restore the field round my head. I spit vomit from my lips. Shrug off the larger shreds of guts, revealing the distraught hell-child. Most of the lice have been knocked from his head. The fire in his eyes has dimmed and he's whimpering softly. I sit up and drag him closer, so he can't escape. I prepare myself to announce him as the true demon thief.

Wait! the voice within me bellows. *This is your final chance. Don't blow it.*

I hesitate, eager to finish this business, but cautious. I wait for the voice to speak again, to give me a clue. But there's only silence. Which is broken by Lord Loss.

"My, my. What now?" he purrs. He's hanging just a few feet overhead. Dervish and Shark are still battling the demons. It's down to us three — me, Lord Loss and the hell-child.

"I keep seeing him everywhere!" I scream, shaking the demon at its master.

"Really?" Lord Loss says, acting surprised. "Then maybe he *is* the thief. Or he might be a red herring, placed by me to throw you off the scent of the real culprit. Or perhaps it's just coincidence and he has nothing to do with anything."

I stare from Lord Loss to the hell-child to Lord Loss again. "Please," I croak. "Help me. Don't make me…"

"What?" Lord Loss asks, not unkindly. "Don't make you choose? But I am not. The choice – whether you make it or not – is entirely yours. There is no time limit. Use your final chance now, if you believe you have caught the one you seek. Otherwise, retreat and try again later. Perhaps you can train the marbles to unmask the thief. Or maybe I'll drop clues for you over the centuries. Or Beranabus might find a way to rescue you."

"All I want is my brother back!" I wail. "Why are you tormenting me like this? What did I ever do to you?"

Lord Loss only smiles in answer then strokes the hell-child's head, calming him. "You hold one of my favourite familiars against his will and mine. It is time to call him a thief or set him free. Gamble or wait. But do it now, before I lose my temper and deny you any real choice." He grins viciously. "Remember how I gave Cadaver a mouth with which to speak? I could just as easily remove yours, robbing you of your chance to name the thief."

I'm crying helplessly. I want to let the hell-child go, delay the moment of naming, give myself time to think. But I know I can't wait. I *know*. Delay it... run... and the chance will never come again. The hell-child will go into hiding, skip ahead of me through the zones of the Board, stay out of my reach no matter how hard I search.

But what if he's not the thief? If he's a decoy, like Lord Loss said, or completely unconnected?

I study the demon through my tears, desperately hoping for some sort of a clue. But there's nothing I haven't seen before, no evidence that he had anything to do with the theft of Art. One last scan, to be on the safe side. His tiny feet, bony legs, skinny body, oversized head. Green skin. The small mouths in his palms, snapping open and closed. The few remaining lice on his head. The orange flames in his otherwise empty sockets.

Nothing about him helps. Guess I'll just have to name him as the thief and hope for...

No. Wait. His eyes.

I stare at the flames. Something about the way they flicker... the colour... but what is it? They remind me of something. Some*one*. I've seen eyes like this before. Not exactly the same, but similar. And only once. But where?

"Come on, Cornelius," Lord Loss encourages me. "Say it quick, before I—"

"Wait!" I roar, clutching the hell-child tighter, shielding him from the demon master. "I'm trying to remember! The eyes! I've seen—"

The hell-child yelps — I must have hurt him when I tightened my grip. With a snarl, he opens his mouth, latches on to my left arm and bites, grey teeth breaking my flesh with ease. I scream and try jerking my arm free, but he has too firm a grip. I reach over with my right hand to prise his jaw loose...

...then stop as though struck by a bolt of red energy.

The biting... the eyes... I remember... the strange hair... the marbles... the large head... orange... I remember... playing with the marbles, holding them up to the light... orange light... finding the hell-child here when we stepped through, when I was searching for my brother... Dad tucking Art and me down beneath the blanket... I *remember*!

And, weak with disbelief, not sure how it can be true, but sickeningly certain that it is, I mutter over the rotten head of the hell-child, "I know who the demon thief is — it's *me*!"

THE THEFT

→Soft pink light swallows me, engulfs the world of guts, blocks everything out. A few seconds of coolness and pinkness, all alone, confusion, uncertainty. Then the light fades and I'm back in Lord Loss's throne room, on my hands and knees in front of the spider-shaped throne, gasping and shivering.

"Kernel!" a woman shouts — Sharmila. She hurries towards me, but Beranabus reaches out and holds her back. The magician's smiling, but a faint frown wrinkles the dirty flesh of his forehead. Shark and Dervish are on their knees close by, sniffing the air and their hands. The stink is gone. That puzzles me, until I remember that only our souls entered the Board. The bodies we inhabited there were fakes. Our real bodies remained in the castle.

Lord Loss is on his throne, the hell-child on his lap, Vein sitting to attention at the base of the throne. No other demons are in the room.

"Say it again, Cornelius," Lord Loss murmurs. "So there can be no doubt."

"I'm the thief," I mutter, still not sure how that can be true. "I stole... I don't know how, but... It was when I was lonely, a year ago. I came here... when I stepped through the window of lights in my bedroom..."

Lord Loss chuckles and bounces the hell-child up and down. "This is *Artery*," he says, "brother of Vein. They are two of my current favourites. Loyal servants, and most amusing when I set them loose on a human. Some time ago, an intruder opened a window into my kingdom. When I peered through it, I found you, Cornelius. I was inclined to take you, to punish you for your impudence. But there was something about the way you faced me and a crackle of unusual magic in the air. I thought it better to wait and observe.

"You came through the window after me. It was outside the castle. Artery was playing nearby, torturing a lesser demon. You grabbed and subdued him, magically transformed him, supplied him with human features, took him to your universe, created a new identity for him and shortened his name to..."

"*Art!*" I croak, more of the memories clicking into place, understanding coming slowly but certainly.

The air around the hell-child shimmers. When it clears, my brother is sitting on the demon master's lap. He gurgles at me, but with Artery's screechy voice. Dim flashes of orange light in his eyes. His messy hair. Head that's slightly too large for his body. His sharp teeth.

"It was when he bit me," I whisper. "That's when I knew. Art loved to bite. And the marbles, when he held them over his eyes — they looked like the demon's."

Lord Loss nods slowly. "You stole him, Cornelius. You were lonely, desperate for a friend, somebody who would be true to you and with you always. You found a way into my kingdom. Snatched Artery. Gave him human shape. Convinced yourself that he was your natural brother."

"But Mum and Dad must have known the truth!" I cry.

"They knew he was not theirs," Lord Loss agrees. "But they did not know he was a demon, where he came from or why you believed he was your brother. He reminded your mother of the baby daughter she lost. She saw him as a second chance, a gift from the gods. Your father wanted to give the baby to the police, to be returned to its rightful parents. He tried to sway Melena, without success. She used *you* to swing him round to her way of thinking. You thought the baby was your brother. If they took him away, she said you'd suffer dreadfully. Out of love for you, he agreed to lie.

"They watched the news closely – furtively – over the coming days. If a baby had been reported missing, perhaps decency would have won out and your father would have handed Art over. Or perhaps not. Your sister's death had hurt him terribly too. Maybe he would have let your mother talk him into holding on to the child, no matter what.

"In any event, when there was no mention of a missing baby, they decided to keep him and rear him as their own, as the brother you believed he was. But they couldn't stay in the city, where people knew they only had one child. So they abandoned their jobs and fled. Took you and the baby away. Started a new life in Paskinston, where nobody had cause to be suspicious, where things were simpler, where they could rear their new son in peace."

He strokes Art's head, never taking his eyes off me. I'm trembling uncontrollably, my world falling to pieces, the last year of my life exposed as a lie, me revealed as a villain, Mum and Dad as devious accomplices.

"How did he transform the demon?" Beranabus asks. "Transfiguration's a complicated spell. He couldn't have managed it alone."

"Yet he did," Lord Loss says. "I assumed he was the pawn of a powerful magician, maybe even a fellow demon. That is why I did not retrieve Artery immediately. I hoped the manipulator of the boy would reveal himself. Eventually, I decided to steal Artery back, hoping to tempt Cornelius's master out of hiding. It was only when Cornelius came into this universe and tested his powers that I realised he'd acted alone. I still do not know how he did it — only that he did."

Everyone's staring at me. I feel like an exhibit at a freak show. *Roll up! Roll up! Come and marvel at Kernel Fleck, thief of demons, master of disguise! He can hide a demon from everybody — even himself!*

"So I never had a brother," I whisper. "It was all a lie."

"A dream," Lord Loss corrects me. "And now you have awoken, thanks to my generous help."

"Some help!" Dervish snorts. "You could have just told him."

"That would have been cheating," Lord Loss says. "He had to discover the truth himself — or search for it in vain for the rest of his life. I would have been happy either way. The misery of his ignorance would have been sweet. But the misery of his understanding is just as welcome."

"What misery?" Shark asks. "He beat you. He found out the truth."

"And lost a brother in the process," Sharmila says softly, as I weep quietly.

"But he never had a brother," Shark says. "It was a sham, a cuckoo's child."

"But Kernel thought it was real." Sharmila frees herself from Beranabus's grip, walks over and lays a hand on my shoulder. Squeezes gently.

"What now?" Beranabus asks, businesslike, no longer interested in the mystery of the theft or the illusion. "Are we free to leave?"

"Of course," Lord Loss says. "Cornelius fulfilled the terms of our agreement. He discovered the true thief and named him. You can depart whenever you like." He looks around absent-mindedly. "Cadaver seems to have slipped away while we were otherwise involved, but I am sure you can track him down again."

"Then let's go," Beranabus says. "We've wasted enough time on this farce."

"Shut up, you stupid, thoughtless man!" Sharmila shouts, surprising us all. She glowers at Beranabus, then strokes the back of my neck. "There is the matter of Kernel's brother to settle."

"*Brother?*" Beranabus huffs. Sharmila points at the child on Lord Loss's knee. "But that's just a demon made up to look like a boy."

"Yes. But he has been Kernel's brother for the past year. And I suspect, by the smile of his master, he can be again. If Kernel so wishes."

Lord Loss laughs hollowly. "You have a sharp eye, Miss Mukherji." He holds Art — Artery — up with four of his hands. The baby giggles and tries to bite off one of the demon master's fingers. "Artery is precious to me, but he has been equally precious to Cornelius. I am not evil-hearted — I have no heart, either evil or good — so I am willing to let my familiar go. If Kernel wishes to take him, I will not stand in his way."

I slowly look up. "I can have Art back? He can be my brother again?"

"If you want," Lord Loss smiles.

I stare at the demon master, then at Art, grinning at me over the lumpy fingers. He looks no different than he did the day Cadaver took him. Why shouldn't I take him home as my brother, carry on with life and try to forget that this mad period of time ever happened?

"What would he be like when he grew up?" Dervish asks.

"Can one ever judge how a child will grow up?" Lord Loss says slyly.

"You know what I mean. Right now he likes biting people. Will he want to do worse things when he's older? Will he be more demon than human? A man on top, a monster beneath?"

"What a way you have with words." Lord Loss shrugs. "I think the true Artery will shine through. Cornelius has the power to shackle him, but not rid him of his origins. He'll want to do terrible things, and will probably find a way to act on his desires. But he will never harm Cornelius, of that I am certain."

Dervish comes over to stand beside Sharmila. He looks at me seriously. "It's your call, Kernel, but I don't think you should take him back. You've seen the way demons behave. You couldn't change him."

"I could try!" I cry. "If I can change his shape, why not his heart?"

"Demons don't experience emotions like we do," Beranabus says softly. "Sometimes they give the impression that they can feel as we feel, care as we care. But they're monsters, all of them. It's their nature. We cannot alter that."

I'm crying hard. I look at Art again, wanting so much to hold him, play with him, grow up with him. It's not fair, having to choose. I'd have been happier if I'd never had a brother. To have him for a year... to come through so much to find him...

only to be faced with *this*… having to go back to the loneliness… tell Mum and Dad I couldn't protect him…

"Maybe I don't care if he kills!" I shout. "Maybe I just don't want to be lonely any more, and having a brother matters to me more than anything else. What if that's the case?"

Beranabus sniffs. "Then good luck to you. Just don't call on my Disciples when the bodies start mounting up. And you might want to tell your parents to stay out of Art's way. They should be safe on the other side of the world."

I howl at Beranabus, Dervish, Lord Loss, Art — the entire world and all the worlds beyond. I hate this universe, both universes, life itself. I wish I could destroy it all, the whole damn lot of it, myself as well. One burst of almighty energy and — *bang!* No more worries or pain.

Then I catch sight of Lord Loss smirking. And Art, smiling innocently, just the slightest twinkle of wickedness in the corner of his eye. I think about Mum and Dad, how they loved me and gave up everything, risking imprisonment and who knows what else, to protect my dark secret and keep me happy. Sure, they did it for themselves too, but I think – believe – they mostly did it for my sake.

And I know I can't do this to them. I can't take a demon in human form into their home and leave it free to strike. I'd be as demonic as Lord Loss if I did that.

"To hell with your rotten familiar!" I moan, turning my back on Lord Loss and the baby-shaped demon. Tears overwhelm me and the world becomes a watery, salty sea. I'm aware of Sharmila hugging me tight, leading me away, the others solemnly following. Lord Loss says something, mocking my misery, but we ignore him. Pass out of the main room, through the other webby chambers, past the room of chess sets, to the drawbridge. Where we pause, just a moment. And I hear, during a gulp between sobs, from deep within the castle, one final childish giggle from the demon Artery — my lost never-brother, Art.

GOODBYES

→Outside the castle. At the point where we entered this world. Beranabus claps my back and says, "Let's go find Cadaver." Sharmila groans. Dervish looks at Beranabus as if he has two heads. Even Shark fidgets as though a terrible curse had been uttered. "What?" Beranabus snaps, frowning at his Disciples. "We have to capture him, squeeze out whatever he knows about the Kah-Gash. That's what we came here for."

"It is over," Sharmila says. "Nadia was wrong about the Kah-Gash. Or we already came upon it and failed to recognise it. Either way, Cadaver's real purpose was to bring Kernel into this universe, so he could learn the truth about the theft. Now it is time for him to return to his parents and—"

"No!" Beranabus shouts. "His brother never mattered. This is about the Kah-Gash and always has been."

"To you, perhaps," Dervish says softly. "But not to Kernel. And not, I think, to the rest of us. Sharmila's right — it's over."

Beranabus glares at us. An angry red flush creeps up his neck. He starts to say something but Shark steps forward, halting him. "I'll serve if you want me. If you think I can help you find this demon-destroying weapon, I'm yours for life. But I doubt I'll make a difference. I don't think any of us will. I agree with Dervish — this was about Kernel and his search. That's what brought us here. It doesn't seem like much, and it's crazy that Raz and Nadia had to die because of it — but that's life."

Beranabus growls. "Think you're smarter than me, do you?"

"No. But I can see the truth when it's sitting before me plain as day. I don't know anything about the Kah-Gash. Maybe you'll find it later, maybe you won't. Maybe Cadaver can lead you to it, maybe he can't. But it's time to let Kernel go. He doesn't belong here. He's not part of this. Not any more."

It's the most I've ever heard Shark say. I want to thank him, but my throat's as tight as when I was being strangled by Cadaver's hairs.

Beranabus scowls at his three Disciples, lets his gaze linger on me, then gives a disinterested sniff. "So be it. I'm not going to argue with all of you. I'm starting to think it *was* a fool's errand. I'll look for Cadaver anyway, just in case, but there's no reason for you to come with me. The fighting's over. And the deaths."

He turns away, takes a deep breath, starts muttering the words of a spell.

Sharmila, Shark and Dervish exchange uncertain glances. "That's it?" Dervish asks. "We can go?"

"Aye. Get the boy to open a window for you. Return to your normal duties. I'll be in touch later. If I need you."

Dervish laughs. Sharmila and Shark smile. Then all three look at me.

"Where do you want to go?" I ask them.

"Drop us off at your place," Shark says. "We'll make our own way from there."

I nod slowly, then face the patches of light. They surround me as usual, now that I've come out of the Board, glowing in the air around me. Half eager, half afraid, I think about Paskinston.

→It doesn't take long. I slot the patches of pulsing lights together. The window opens. Clean blue light. The doorway out of all this craziness. I take one last look back at the castle, the demon-laced sky, Beranabus.

"Thank you," I mutter. "I know you only helped me because you wanted to find the Kah-Gash. But I couldn't have discovered the truth without you."

"Much good it did you," Beranabus grunts. He looks at me with his grey-blue eyes. Cocks his head. "Home isn't always where you expect it to be. It can change, as life changes. If you ever need me, you know where to find me."

"He won't," Dervish says shortly, then pushes me through the window of light, out of the universe of demons.

* * *

→Night. We're in a field outside Paskinston. Where Mrs Egin exploded and Cadaver crossed. The four of us standing beneath a half moon, looking at each other, breathing in the delicious smell of our own world.

"We are a sight," Sharmila laughs, nodding at our torn clothes, ripped flesh and bare feet.

"At least we're not a stench," Shark says. He sniffs a sleeve and his face turns green at the memory of the gory pool.

"Thank you," I whisper, eyes lowered, suddenly shy, feeling like a child again, the way I did before I crossed universes. I was their equal over there. Here, I'm just a boy.

"No need for thanks," Dervish smiles. "We had the adventure of a lifetime."

"I would not call it an adventure," Sharmila says thoughtfully. "More a nightmare — the like of which I hope never to experience again."

Dervish smiles. "Be truthful. Now we've come through alive, don't tell me you aren't a bit sorry that it's over. It was wild but magical. Right?"

"No. It was horrible. I hated every minute of it."

"Shark?" Dervish asks.

"I hated the pool of slime," he grunts and we all laugh. "Otherwise, it was a buzz. But that's because we survived. I'm sure Raz and Nadia had a different view of it."

I feel a jolt of guilt when he mentions Nadia. I should tell them about her. But I gave my word. Besides, she said she wouldn't hurt them. The only one she hates is Beranabus.

"What was Raz like?" Dervish asks, smile fading.

"A gentleman," Sharmila says.

"Yeah," Shark agrees. "I knew Raz. A top cat. But let's not talk about him. In our business, it's best to forget about death and focus on living." He stretches and groans. "I'm off to find a lake to soak in. How about you lot?"

"I'll come with you," Dervish says. "I still have a lot to learn about being a Disciple."

"I'm not so sure," Shark murmurs, then raises an eyebrow at Sharmila.

"I want some time off," the Indian lady says, gazing at the moon. "I have been a Disciple for many years. I am due a break. Maybe I will go to the village of my parents and pray to their memory. They were killed by demons." She sighs and lowers her eyes. "I will pray for Raz too. And Nadia. And the others who died in the course of this quest." She looks at me. "And I will pray for Kernel. And maybe for Art, even if he did not ever really exist."

I smile at Sharmila thankfully, then stretch out my arms for a hug. As she wraps her arms around me, she whispers in my ear. "It was strange that you could not find the Kah-Gash."

"Maybe it doesn't exist," I reply.

"Or maybe…" She hesitates, then releases me. "I wonder what would have happened if you'd tried to open a window to one of us when we were with you in that universe."

I frown. "What do you mean?"

She smiles cryptically in answer, kisses my cheeks, then steps back.

"We can stay with you a while," Dervish says, as I hover uncertainly at the edge of the village. "Help you readjust and explain all this to your parents."

I laugh. "You really think you can explain Lord Loss to my mum and dad?"

"You have a point," Dervish chuckles.

I shake Shark's hand, admiring his tattoos one final time. He salutes sharply when I let go. Then I shake hands with Dervish. "Your spikes have gone floppy," I note.

"I feel floppy all over," he grins.

The four of us share one final glance that says more than any words. With a tired wave, I turn away from the three Disciples, face the village lights, steady myself and wonder what Mum and Dad will say when I step through the door. With an excited but nervous shiver, I start on the short walk home.

HOME ALONELY

→It wasn't a glorious homecoming.

Nearly seven years had passed since I stepped through the window in search of Art. I found it almost impossible to believe, even though Lord Loss had warned me. Seven years of change, births and deaths, the world moving on — and I missed every minute of it.

Mum and Dad looked a lot older than I remembered. Wrinklier, greyer, a sadness in their eyes that hadn't been there before.

They thought I was a ghost. Although seven years had slipped by, I looked exactly the way I did when I disappeared, even dressed in the same clothes. Mum screamed. Dad too. They spun away from me, covering their eyes, panting with terror.

I hadn't expected such a reaction or prepared myself for the experience of having Mum and Dad scream at me with horror. I fell apart. Collapsed in tears. "It's me!" I kept wailing. "It's me! Me! *Me!*"

Eventually, shaking with fear, Dad edged forward. Maybe he wouldn't have been so brave if I hadn't been crying like a baby. He poked my bald head, finger trembling, expecting it to slide through me. When it didn't, he frowned and poked me again.

"I'm real," I moaned, looking at him, wanting him to hold me, hug me, tell me he loved me. "It's me. Kernel. I'm real, Dad. I'm back."

"Kernel?" he croaked, shaking his head softly. "It can't be. You're... no... it can't..."

Then he fell on me, folded me in his arms, bellowed my name and burst into tears. Moments later, Mum was beside me too, the pair picking at me, poking me, clutching me. Crying and laughing at the same time.

→I spent ages trying to explain. I told them about the lights, the window, the kidnapping, stepping through after Cadaver, Beranabus, my journey between worlds, Lord Loss, Artery. They didn't believe me. Couldn't. But they had no other explanation for how I'd turned up unchanged (except for lots of cuts, scars and bruises).

"We should take him to a doctor," Dad said. "Have his body and mind looked at by experts. They might be able to uncover the truth."

"No!" Mum hissed before I could insist that my story *was* the truth. "He'd be a freak. There'd be questions we don't want to answer. They'd take him away. We might never see him again, lose him like Annabella and..." She didn't say the name of her third child. She refused to discuss Art not being real. Dad didn't probe either. It was the one part of my story neither asked to hear a second time.

With no other option, they reluctantly accepted my outlandish tales. But they didn't tell the neighbours about me. Dad said we'd be treated as lunatics if I repeated my demonic stories. Also, a lot of the people of Paskinston had lost children when Cadaver attacked. He wasn't sure how my reappearance would affect them.

They hid me inside the house while they tried to think of a way to introduce me back into village life. Mum wanted to pretend I was an orphaned cousin who just happened to look a lot like their supposedly dead son. Dad played about with a deep-freeze theory — he thought he could convince people that I'd been kept on ice by scientists for the past seven years.

When they realised how weak those explanations sounded, they decided to simply leave without saying anything. Running away had worked once — why not a second time? Pack our bags, move to where nobody knew us, start afresh. Mum and Dad loved Paskinston, but they loved me more. Stealing away like thieves in the night, saying nothing to any of their friends, seemed like the only solution. So that's what we did.

→After trying out some small towns, where Mum never felt easy, we ended up in a city. Dad found work on a construction site, Mum in a fast-food restaurant. They teach me when they come home at night. During the day I stay indoors, watching television, reading, playing games, making model aeroplanes. It's not safe for me to go out and interact with other people. Mum and Dad are afraid I'll be taken from them if the truth emerges.

I'm not enjoying this life. It's not how I thought it would be. I did a brave thing, risked all to save my brother, went through torments and overcame obstacles that most people couldn't even imagine. But I'm not allowed to talk about it. I have to keep it hidden, like something shameful. We don't even talk about Art, what happened to him, the fact that he was a demon in disguise. I tried discussing it with Mum once, but she clapped her hands over her ears and shrieked at me to shut up and never mention his name again.

Mum and Dad aren't happy either. They don't say so, but I can see that secretly they wish I'd never returned. Losing me and Art was hard, but after seven years they'd learnt to deal with it. They'd found peace in Paskinston, were getting on with life, grateful to have each other and a place to call home.

I've wrecked all that. Turned their world upside-down and inside out. Forced them to abandon their home and friends, take to the road, live a life of secrets and fear.

I didn't want to ruin their lives. I wanted to save Art, bring him home, be a hero. I wanted Mum and Dad to hold me and love me, for everything to be all right after that terrible universe of monsters. I wanted my life back.

Instead, I've returned to lies and disguise, a nightmare every bit as awful as the one I hoped to escape for ever when I left the universe of the Demonata.

→The loneliness is worse than ever. Trapped indoors most of the time, nobody to play with or speak to. It was bad enough when I felt like an outsider, but at least I could mingle with other children, go to school, act like I fitted in. Now I'm totally alone. I can't even talk with Mum or Dad. They're always uneasy around me. They love me because I'm their son, but I'm sure they wonder sometimes and ask themselves, "Is that really Kernel? Can it truly be the boy we thought we'd lost? Or is it some monster pretending to be him?"

They have nightmares. I've heard them moaning in their sleep. Sometimes, one will wake screaming and sob for hours, held by the other, comforted.

But they never hold or comfort me.

→Out of boredom, I start experimenting with the patches of light. Curious to see if I can manipulate them. Trying to get them to pulse. I don't want to open a window. I just want to see if I have the power here.

For a long time I make no progress. But eventually, I find a way. I have to think about a specific spot in the

Demonata's universe, somewhere I've been. That gets the lights pulsing, though it takes hours of concentration. Once they're going, if I think of another place or person, other patches pulse, but slowly, in small numbers. I'm sure I could get more of them to pulse if I pushed myself, and gradually build a window. If I wanted to. Which I don't. Why would I ever return to that universe of vicious, magical insanity?

→A dark, wet day. Mum and Dad are out at work. They were awake most of last night, crying and talking. I hate seeing them unhappy. I've tried everything I can to cheer them up and make it easier. Told jokes, avoided mentioning demons, worked hard at my lessons, kept up a smile whenever they're around.

But nothing works. They were delighted when I first returned, but that quickly gave way to a confused sadness and they're getting sadder every day. They don't know how to deal with me or this new life they've found themselves part of. It's too complicated.

They're starting to resent me. I can see it in their eyes, just a flash, every so often. A look that says they wish I'd never come back. That look strikes at my heart every time I catch it. Makes me want to burst into tears and throw myself at them for a hug. But I hold my smile. Pretend not to notice. Act like everything's fine. And only cry when they're not around.

*   *   *

→The clouds part shortly after midday, for a few minutes. Then they roll back together and rain comes down more heavily than before.

Thinking about the universe of the Demonata. I hated it there, but I didn't feel out of place. I had a purpose, a function. I was the equal of Sharmila, Dervish, Raz, Shark, Nadia. No good at fighting, but I had other talents. They respected me. Even Beranabus was impressed.

I remember what he said. "Home isn't always where you expect it to be. You know where to find me."

Crazy. As if I'd ever want to go back there, face demons again, live like Nadia, a slave of the magician. Adrift in a universe of horrors, where you can't even depend on time. Nothing in this world could be as bad as that. Mum and Dad will accept me eventually. I'll make friends. Grow up normally. We'll laugh about this one day.

I'm sitting on the floor in the small living room of the apartment which we're renting. I rise and walk to the bathroom. Take the marbles out of my pocket, the orange marbles which I've carried ever since Art was stolen. I look down at them then hold them up, standing before the mirror. Place them in front of my eyes. Watch them twinkle. I try directing magic into them. Take my fingers away, telling them to hover in the air.

They fall. Roll away. I hurry after them before they disappear down one of the holes in the old floorboards.

Back to the living room, remembering how magical I was in that other place, the things I could do, the power I had. Sitting on the couch, I study the marbles again and recall what Sharmila said to me in the field before we parted. I think I know now what she was hinting, the secret she suspected. It's an impossible, wild and crazy theory. I'm sure it can't be right. But if it is...

Trying not to worry too much about what that might mean, I put the marbles away. As I stand, I notice some of the lights around me pulsing slowly. I stare at them numbly. It's like they're calling me, trying to suck me back into that realm of madness.

I turn my back on them and stride around the tiny apartment, looking for something to distract me. End up in my Mum and Dad's bedroom. Not much bigger than mine. A bed they can only just fit into. I let my eyes drift. It's untidy, clothes thrown about the place, dirty socks and underwear. The rooms were never like this in our previous homes. Mum was house-proud. Dad too. Always cleaning and tidying away. But not any more.

The mess upsets me. I turn to leave, but spot the corner of something sticking out from under a pillow on the bed. I edge over and slide it all the way out. It's a photograph of me and Art. I haven't seen it before. I'm holding Art over my head. He's laughing. I think I'm laughing too. But it's difficult to tell. Because Mum has scrawled all over my face with a pen. Line after line of black ink, obliterating my features, scratching me out of existence.

I put the photo back in its place. Cover it entirely. Return to the living room, my stomach hard and cold. The lights are pulsing around me, lots of them, faster than before, like they used to in the Demonata's universe. I think about Beranabus, what Sharmila said, the bitter look I sometimes get from Mum and Dad, the photo.

As a single tear trickles down my cheek, I reach out like a robot and start slotting the patches of pulsing lights together.

KAH-GASH

→Beranabus is waiting in a surprisingly scenic spot, lying on a pile of deep green grass next to a waterfall, beneath the shelter of a leafy tree. The only hint that this is another universe — blood, not water, flows from the waterfall.

"I thought you might come looking for me," he says, sounding more sad than smug. "I decided to rest here a while." He looks around. "I come here often. My mother liked this place. I feel close to her here."

"Was your mother a magician?" I ask.

"Not as such." He stares at the waterfall, stroking the petals of a fresh flower which he's pinned to his jacket. "She died not long after I was born. I used magic to find out about her later – that's how I learnt about this spot – but I never knew her when I was a child. As for my father…"

He snorts, then says with unusual softness, "I know what it's like to be lonely. To have no family. To feel out of place in the world. I hate myself for what I did to Nadia and for what I'm asking of you. I know how wretched her life was and what you're suffering now, because I've felt that way myself.

I'd have spared you both if I could. But the universe demands sacrifice and pain of its champions. When there's no other way… when the fate of billions hangs in the balance… what choice do we have?"

I stare at the ancient magician, not sure how to answer. Before I can think of something to say, he barks a laugh, pushes himself to his feet and smiles, more like his old cynical self. "Come to be my assistant, have you? Couldn't fit in with the folks at home? Normal life not for you any more?"

"You knew I'd return, didn't you?" I accuse him.

"I've lived and seen enough to know how difficult it is to settle for a small life when you're destined for greatness. The universe created you for a reason, Kernel Fleck, and it wasn't to waste your time in an ordinary job, among everyday people. Destiny is a determined opponent. Not many get the better of it."

"So what now?" I ask. "Do we go after Cadaver?"

"I don't think so." Beranabus frowns. "I'm angling more towards the idea of re-tracing the route he followed when he was on his way to Lord Loss's. Maybe we'll find something on one of the worlds he visited, or on a world we bypassed when you opened the window directly to him."

"Or maybe…" I stop, not wanting to say it. The window behind me has faded, but I could easily build another if I wanted. Find my parents. Try again. It's not too late to change my mind. But if I tell Beranabus of my suspicions, I can never return. I'll be his — the universe's — for life.

Beranabus studies me with one eyebrow raised, smiling as if nothing I say can take him by surprise, like he's waiting for me to make a suggestion so that he can say he's already thought of it.

I chew my lower lip, trying to make up my mind. I think about the photo again. Shiver then straighten up and put my theory to the test.

"I'm picturing Cadaver inside my head now," I tell Beranabus then look around. "Dozens of lights are flashing. I could open a window to him if I wanted."

I clear the demon from my thoughts and think about Beranabus. "Now I've got *you* in my head." My stomach sinks when I check the lights and my worst fears are realised. "Nothing's happening. No lights are pulsing."

"Of course not," he snorts. "I'm here with you. There's no need to open a window to find me."

"Right. Now I'll think about a waterfall on Earth — Niagara Falls." I concentrate. "Lots of pulsing lights again. But when I think about that waterfall of blood... nothing."

Bernabus is frowning. "What are you—"

"Picturing Sharmila," I interrupt. "Dervish. Shark. Lights pulse for all three of them." And for Nadia too, though I don't tell Beranabus that. "Now I'm thinking of myself — no flashing lights. And now... now I'm thinking about the Kah-Gash." I give it a full minute. Two. Five. Eyes shut, focusing hard, saying the word over and over. When I finally open my eyes, none of the lights are pulsing, and Beranabus is staring at me, trembling slightly.

"Nobody knows what the Kah-Gash was," the magician says softly, "or what sort of parts it was broken down into. I've always assumed the pieces would be power-charged stones or other objects of energy, but I guess they could be hidden in anything. Even in…"

"people." I finish, then take a deep breath. "The piece of the Kah-Gash… the weapon that can destroy universes… We've been close to it all along. Too close to recognise it. It's here now. It always has been."

Beranabus shudders, then steels himself. "Am I the one?"

"No," I say sadly. "I think it's *me.*"

DARREN SHAN

SLAWTER
BOOK THREE OF THE DEMONATA

Nightmares haunt the dreams of Dervish O'Grady since his return from the Demonata universe, but Grubbs takes care of his uncle as they both try to continue a normal, demon-free existence. When a legendary cult director calls in Dervish as consultant for a new horror movie, it seems a perfect excuse for a break from routine and a chance for some fun.

But being on the set of a town called Slawter stirs up more than memories for Grubbs and his friend Bill-E.

Lights… camera… *Slawter!*

Sneak preview…

→The end of a typical school day. Yawning through classes, desperate for lunch-time so I could hang out with my friends and chat about movies, music, TV, computer games, whatever. Bill-E joined us for some of it. I don't spend as much time with Bill-E as I used to. He doesn't fit in with my new friends — they think he's geekish. They don't slag him off when I'm around, but I know they do when I'm not. I feel bad about that and try to help Bill-E relax so they can see his real side. But he gets nervous around the others, acts differently, becomes the butt of their jokes.

Thinking about Bill-E as I walk home. I don't want us to stop being friends. He's my brother and he was really good to me when I first moved here. But it's difficult because I don't want to lose my new friends either. Guess I'll just have to work harder to make him feel like part of the group. Try and be like one of those TV kids who always solve their problems by the end of the show.

Dervish is sitting on the stairs when I let myself in. I'm dripping wet — it's been pouring for the last couple of hours. Normally, when the weather's bad, he picks me up on his motorbike. When there was no sign of him today, I figured his mood hadn't improved since breakfast. I was right. He's as blank as he was this morning, staring off into space, not registering me until I'm right in front of him.

"Dervish! Hey, Derveeshio! Earth to Dervish! Are you reading me, captain?"

He blinks, frowns as if he doesn't know who I am, then smiles. "Grubbs. You're alive. I thought…" His expression clears. "Sorry. I was miles away."

I sit beside him. "Bad day?"

"Can't remember," he replies. "Why are you home early?" I hold up my watch and tap it. Dervish reads the time. Sighs. "I'm losing it, Grubbs."

My insides tighten, but I don't let Dervish see my fear. "Losing what — your sanity? You can't lose what you never had."

"My grip." Dervish looks down at his feet, bare and dirty. "I wasn't like this before. I wasn't this distracted and empty. Was I?" He looks at me pleadingly.

"You've been through hell, Derv," I tell him quietly. "You can't expect to recover without a few hiccups."

"I know. But I wasn't this way, right? Some days I can't remember. I feel like it's always been like this."

"No," I say firmly. "It's just a phase. It'll pass."

"All things must pass," Dervish mutters. Then he looks at me sideways, his cool blue eyes coming into focus. "Why are you wet?"

"Took a bath. Forgot to strip." I rap his forehead with my knuckles, then point to the windows and the rain battering the panes. "Numbnuts."

"Oh," Dervish says. "I should have picked you up."

"No worries." I rise and stretch, dripping steadily. "I'm going up to shower and change into dry clothes. I'll stick this lot in to wash. Anything you want me to add?" I did all the jobs around the house when Dervish was a vegetable. Hard to break the habit.

"No, I don't think so. I..." Dervish stares at his left hand. There's a black mark on it, a small 'd'. "There was something I meant to tell you. What...?" He clicks his fingers. "I had a phone call, a follow-up to some e-mails I've been getting recently. Ever heard of someone called Davida Haym?"

"No, can't say..." I pause. "Hold on. Not David A Haym, the movie producer?"

"That's her."

"I thought that was a guy."

"Nope. She uses David A on her movies, but it's Davida. You know about her?"

"Sure. She makes horror movies. *Zombie Zest. Witches Weird. Night Mayors* — that's, like, *Nightmares*, only two words. It's about evil mayors who band together to set up a meat production plant, only the meat they process is human flesh."

"Win many Oscars?" Dervish asks.

"Swept the board," I chuckle. "I can't believe she's a woman. I always thought... But what about her? I didn't think you were into horror flicks."

"She phoned me earlier."

I do a double-take. "David A Haym called you?"

"Davida Haym. Yes." Dervish squints at me. "Have I grown a second head?"

"Hell, it's *David A Haym*, Dervish! That's like saying Steven Spielberg was on the line, or George Lucas. OK, not as big as those, but still…"

"I didn't know she was famous," Dervish says. "She told me the names of some of her movies, but I don't watch a lot of films. She made it sound like she was a cult director."

"She is. She doesn't make films with big-name stars. But her movies are great! Anyone who loves horror knows about David A Haym. Though I'm not sure many know she's a woman."

"That's a big sticking point for you, isn't it?" Dervish grins. "You're not turning into a chauvinist, are you?"

"No, I just…" I shake my head. Water flies from my ginger hair and splatters the wall. "What did she want?"

"She's making a new movie. Asked if she could meet me. She'd heard I know a lot about the occult. Wants to pick my brain." He tweaks his chin, forgetting the beard isn't there. "I hope she didn't mean that literally."

"Did you say yes?" I ask, excited.

"Said I'd think about it."

"Dervish! You've got to! It's David A Haym! Did she say she'd come here? Can I meet her? Do you think—"

"Easy, tiger," Dervish laughs. "We didn't discuss where we'd meet. But you think I should agree to it?"

"Absolutely!"

"Then meet we shall," Dervish says, getting to his feet and heading up to his office. "Anything to please Master Grady."

I tramp up the stairs after him, pulling off my clothes, thinking about how cool it would be if I could meet David A Haym... and also how weird it is that one of the world's premier horror producers is a woman.

DARREN SHAN
LORD LOSS

BOOK ONE OF THE DEMONATA

When Grubbs Grady first encounters Lord Loss and his evil minions, he learns three things:

- the world is vicious,
- magic is possible,
- demons are real.

He thinks that he will never again witness such a terrible night of death and darkness.

…He is wrong.

Also available on audio, read by Rupert Degas

PB ISBN 0 00 719320 3
CD ISBN 0 00 721389 1

DARREN SHAN
CIRQUE DU FREAK

THE SAGA OF DARREN SHAN
BOOK 1

Darren Shan is just an ordinary schoolboy – until he gets an invitation to visit the Cirque Du Freak… until he meets Madam Octa… until he comes face to face with a creature of the night.

Soon, Darren and his friend Steve are caught in a deadly trap. Darren must make a bargain with the one person who can save Steve. But that person is not human and only deals in blood…

ISBN 0 00 675416-3

www.darrenshan.com

DARREN SHAN

THE VAMPIRE'S ASSISTANT

THE SAGA OF DARREN SHAN
BOOK 2

Darren Shan was just an ordinary schoolboy – until his visit to the Cirque Du Freak. Now, as he struggles with his new life as a Vampire's Assistant, he tries desperately to resist the one thing that can keep him alive… blood. But a gruesome encounter with the Wolf Man may change all that…

ISBN 0 00 675513-5

www.darrenshan.com

DARREN SHAN
TUNNELS OF BLOOD

THE SAGA OF DARREN SHAN
BOOK 3

Darren Shan, the Vampire's Assistant, gets a taste of city life when he leaves the Cirque Du Freak with Evra and Mr Crepsley. At night the vampire goes about secret business, while by day Darren enjoys his freedom.

But then bodies are discovered... Corpses drained of blood... The hunt for the killer is on and Darren's loyalties are tested to the limit as he fears the worst. One mistake and they are all doomed to perish in the tunnels of blood...

ISBN 0 00 675514-3

www.darrenshan.com